DISASTER...

You know how in movies sometimes they'll switch to slow motion so you can see every-thing clearly? That's what the next split second was like for me. Clearly, I saw Emerson stumble over his own feet. Clearly, I saw the cup fly from his hand. Clearly, I saw it coming right at me. Clearly, I saw it all, but could do absolutely nothing to stop it, since I was in s-l-o-w m-o-t-i-o-n, too.

Then that cold water hit my lap and every-thing went from slow motion to hyperspeed. I jumped up. "Oh no!" It looked like I'd wet my pants.

A Georgia Book Award Finalist

OTHER BOOKS YOU MAY ENJOY

ATTACK

OF THE

MUTANT
UNDERWEAR

TOM BIRDSEYE

PUFFIN BOOKS

PUFFIN

Published by the Penguin Group

Penguin Young Readers Group, 345 Hudson Street, New York, New York 10014, U.S.A.
Penguin Group (Canada), 90 Eglinton Avenue East, Suite 700, Toronto, Ontario, Canada M4P 2Y3
(a division of Pearson Penguin Canada Inc.)
Penguin Books Ltd, 80 Strand, London WC2R 0RL, England
Penguin Ireland, 25 St Stephen's Green, Dublin 2, Ireland (a division of Penguin Books Ltd)
Penguin Group (Australia), 250 Camberwell Road, Camberwell, Victoria 3124, Australia
(a division of Pearson Australia Group Pty Ltd)
Penguin Books India Pvt Ltd, 11 Community Centre, Panchsheel Park, New Delhi - 110 017, India
Penguin Group (NZ), Cnr Airborne and Rosedale Roads, Albany, Auckland 1310, New Zealand
(a division of Pearson New Zealand Ltd)
Penguin Books (South Africa) (Pty) Ltd, 24 Sturdee Avenue, Rosebank,
Johannesburg 2196, South Africa

Registered Offices: Penguin Books Ltd, 80 Strand, London WC2R 0RL, England

First published in the United States of America by Holiday House, 2003
Published by Puffin Books, a division of Penguin Young Readers Group, 2006

1 3 5 7 9 10 8 6 4 2

LIBRARY OF CONGRESS CATALOGING-IN-PUBLICATION DATA

Birdseye, Tom.
Attack of the mutant underwear / Tom Birdseye.
p. cm.
Summary: Fifth-grader Cody Carson keeps a journal of his hopes for a
fresh start in a town where nobody knows about his humiliating mistakes
of the past, but before school even begins so does his embarrassment.
ISBN 0-14-240734-8 (pbk.)
[1. Schools—Fiction. 2. Interpersonal relations—Fiction. 3. Embarrassment—Fiction.
4. Diaries—Fiction. 5. Humorous stories.] I. Title.
PZ7.B5213At 2006 [Fic]—dc22 2006041600

Printed in the United States of America

To Amy T.
Wonder Girl!

ATTACK
OF THE
MUTANT
UNDERWEAR

Monday, September 4
Labor Day

Hear Ye, Hear Ye! Listen Up, Everybody!

I, Cody Lee Carson, have an announcement to make. As of this exact moment (drumroll, please), I have resolved to become (louder drumroll) a changed man!

That's right. No more embarrassing mistakes, like when I got my head stuck in the school bus window.

No more bozo-brained mess-ups, like the time I dived out of the maple tree with a bungee cord hooked to my belt.

No more trips to the principal's office, or bad grades, or missed recesses, or being grounded for stuff I really didn't mean to do.

That was the *old* Cody Lee Carson. Today another Cody Lee Carson has magically appeared—tah-dah!—the very cool New Me!

And this is my New Me Journal, page one, numero uno. In which I will write the story of my New Life here in my New, Nobody-Knows-About-the-Old-Cody town of Benton, Oregon. That way, after I take full advantage of this second chance, and everybody is wondering how I turned into such an incredible, amazing superstar and ace-brilliant-type-author-guy, they can just read this and they'll know the whole story.

So remember, whoever you are who found this ordinary-looking journal (probably in a trunk in some dusty attic), you're holding a priceless piece of history in your hands. DON'T DROP IT!

But on with my New Life. Where was I? Oh yeah, I was about to explain how moving to a place where nobody knows you can actually be the best, especially when—oops, gotta go. Mom is calling. But don't worry, I'm not in trouble. I didn't do anything stupid or wrong. That was the Old Me, remember? Mom is just ready to go shopping, that's all. Got to get my New Clothes so I can start fifth grade at my New School looking like—you guessed it—the New Me.

Don't change that channel while I'm gone, though, Cody Lee Carson fans. Stay right here, okay? Good! Now I've REALLY got to hightail it. Mom is beeping the horn.

Later!

Still Monday, September 4
Labor Day

What do you get if you spell *Mom* backward?

You get the same thing you started with, that's what. M-O-M turned around is still M-O-M. Just like my M-O-M can still be a pain when she wants to be.

You'd think that after I told her about the New Me, she'd treat her one and only son with all the honor and respect I clearly deserve.

You'd think.

It all started in the boys' section at Mattingly's Department Store. We were almost finished shopping for school. Things had gone pretty well, until Mom decided she did *not* want to buy me a pair of Imadude jeans.

"Too expensive," she said. "All that money for a fancy label." She had that look on her face. (You know, like she's totally made up her mind and there is nothing I can do about it, no way, no how.) It seemed hopeless.

Until my little five-year-old sister, Molly (I call her Molly the Creature, or MC, for short), started complaining that she wanted to exchange her new white socks for black ones because they'd never get dirty. "Black socks!" she sang loud enough for everyone in Mattingly's to hear. "They never get dirty, the longer you wear them, the stiffer they get. Sometimes I think of the laundry, but something inside me says, 'Not yet, not yet!'"

Normally, Mom just ignores Molly when she acts like a creature. But today, for some reason, she couldn't. And the next thing I knew, MC was picking out a bunch of black socks.

Which gave me—aha!—an opening. I pointed out to Mom that in order to be fair, I should now be able to pick whatever kind of pants I wanted. Mom rolled her eyes but said, "Okay." I grinned and went straight for the Imadudes to try them on.

But Mom wasn't done with me yet. I was admiring my new jeans in front of the dressing room mirror when she piped up from outside the door, "Do they fit all right?"

I looked myself over. "They fit great." They made me look like a New Me man, a manly New Me man who knows what he wants out of life—fame and fortune, for starters—and how to get it. I struck a manly New Me man pose and flexed my manly New Me man muscles.

"But do they have room for you to grow?" Mom asked.

"Yep," I said. "They're cool."

"Around the waist?"

I let out a big sigh, and wondered, Just what is it with moms? Are they born this way, or do their brains fall apart when they hit middle age? "The jeans are fine," I mumbled, "just fine. Let's get them." And I started to take my new Imadudes off so we could buy them.

"How about length?"

"Yes, Mom."

"You're sure?"

"Yes, Mom. I already told you."

"Let me see."

Jeans down to my knees, I jumped. "No, Mom, I'm not—"

But she had already opened the dressing room door. Past which, at that exact moment, a *girl* was leading a little boy toward another dressing room.

Yes, a girl, as in female-type person.

"Mom!" I screeched. But it was too late.

The *girl* had seen me.

Seen me in my underwear.

And—*poof!*—it was like I was the Old Me again, back in Portland during our fourth-grade Oregon history play, *Westward Ho!* Halfway through my entrance, my pioneer suspenders decided they'd had enough of holding up my pioneer pants. Which dropped south and got tangled around my legs. The next thing I knew, I was flying through the air like Superman. I skidded to a stop right there in front of everybody—kids, teachers, parents— my Tweety Bird underwear shining in the spotlights.

I got teased for weeks. "Hey, here comes Tweety Bird Butt!" kids would say. "Haw! Haw!" Or "Look! It's a bird! It's a plane! No, it's Super-Tweety! Haw! Haw!"

I threw every pair of Looney Tunes underwear I owned in the garbage the day we moved from Portland. And I was sure I'd gotten rid of my Old Me bad-luck past along with them.

Until this afternoon, that is. The girl at Mattingly's didn't laugh at me, or say a word. In fact, she turned her head and acted like she hadn't seen a thing. Still, I've got an Old Me yucky feeling way down deep in the pit of my stomach that just won't go away.

Tuesday, September 5

Last spring I read a bumper sticker on a car that said, "Some days you eat the bear. Some days the bear eats you." Which I figure means that you never know what life is going to dish up from one day to the next, or how it will all turn out in the end.

Like today, for example. I woke up at dawn in a cold sweat. I'd dreamed that I was at my new school in my new class, all set to start my New Life as the New Me. But then I turned around and there was the girl from Mattingly's—same brown hair and glasses. Instead of acting like she hadn't spotted me with my pants down, though, she started yelling, "See, I told you! He's in his underwear!"

It was true. There I sat on the first day of fifth grade wearing nothing but a pair of my old Tweety Birds. They'd come back from the garbage grave to haunt me. "No!" I screamed. But there was no hiding. The kids pointed and laughed. "Look, he's in his underwear! Haw! Haw!"

No way could I get back to sleep after a dream like that. I pulled my blanket over my head and squeezed my eyes shut, but it was no use. Bear breath was hot on the back of my neck.

Still, what was I going to do, stay home under the covers? Not if Mom and Dad had anything to do with it. "Get up, Cody," they said. "It's the first day of school!" So I did, and put on some very plain white underwear and my New Me Imadude jeans, and a T-shirt that says "Just Do It!," and went downstairs.

As soon as I walked into the kitchen, MC peered over the top of a Cheerios box and said, "It's your turn to clean out the kitty litter."

In as calm and controlled a voice as I could manage, I said, "No, it's *your* turn. You're just trying to get out of it because you're afraid of Emma."

"I am not!" MC said, scowling.

"Yes, you are," I said. "That's why you stand

up on the toilet seat to brush your teeth. You're afraid Emma is going to attack you."

"I like standing on the toilet seat!" MC insisted. "I do it all the time. It's fun! It's *your* turn to clean out the litter box!"

For a minute I gave some serious thought to beaning my little sister with a grapefruit. But then I remembered my dream, and that bad feeling in my gut, and those bumper sticker bears, and I thought, Don't push your luck, Cody. So I said, "Okay, I'll do it."

MC grinned from ear to ear and said, "When I grow up, I'm going to be allergic to kitty litter!"

I couldn't help it: I laughed. And for a minute that weird feeling in the pit of my stomach eased off and I thought that maybe, just maybe, it would turn out to be a good day after all.

By the time Mom and Dad had driven us to Garfield Elementary School, though, I was worrying again. MC kept singing, "I know a song that gets on everybody's nerves, everybody's nerves, everybody's nerves. I know a song that gets on everybody's nerves, and this is how it goes." Over and over she sang it, and it worked. It really got on my nerves.

Then Mom insisted that we all walk MC to class. "It's her first day of kindergarten, ever!"

So much for starting my New Life by entering my new school like a real fifth grader. In I walked with my parents. I did my best to act like I didn't know them, and stay cool. Until we'd dropped MC off and Mom said, "Now we can escort Cody to his room!"

"No!" I said. "I can get there on my own!"

Mom started to argue, but Dad stopped her. "How about we just walk him as far as the big kids' hall? Then he can go the rest of the way by himself."

Which is exactly what we did, and the next thing I knew I was standing by my New Me self outside of my classroom. On the door was a little plaque with the name of my teacher— Ms. Bitnerinski.

Aw, man. I had no idea how to pronounce a name like that. Then I saw the piece of paper taped below it: "Better known as Ms. B."

Ah! *That* I could handle.

Another piece of paper was taped farther down.

Please try to remember:

—More learning takes place when you are awake.

—It's not helpful to yell "He's dead!" when roll is being taken.

—Hamsters, particularly Ralph, cannot fly.

—Being a fifth grader does not put you in charge of the school.

—It's best not to dissect things unless instructed.

—Ralph will not morph if you squeeze him hard enough.

—Funny noises are not funny, unless made by Ms. B.

—Ms. B does not accept bribes . . .

At the bottom, in print so small I had to squint to read it, was written:

. . . except in the form of chocolate.

"Ha!" A big laugh popped out of my mouth just as the classroom door swung open. There stood Ms. B, glaring down at me.

"You think that's funny, huh?"

But before I could panic, she smiled. "Welcome! You must be Cody. Come on in! You can take that seat in the back on the left."

I looked to where she was pointing, and my stomach dropped. Sitting right behind the empty chair was the girl from Mattingly's. I turned to run, like you would from a hungry bear. But then a wide-bodied kid whose name turned out to be Emerson raised his hand and said to Ms. B, "He could sit here instead. I could move back there." And in a blink I was in the front row, far from the girl from Mattingly's. Whew!

Which is pretty much how the whole day went. Every time something seemed like it was going to go Old Cody wrong, and I was sure the New Me would soon be nothing but bear bait, I'd scoot out of the trap like it had no teeth at all.

Even in reading group, when I was sitting right across from the girl from Mattingly's (her name is Amy), and I looked up from my book to see her staring at me. I thought, She's going to blab to everybody! But she didn't say a word.

Whew-double-whew! My nightmare didn't come true. The bear didn't eat me. I survived my first day at my new school. No, I did better than survive. I *aced* it!

But, man, am I tired. Being the New Me wears a guy out. My hand aches, too, from all this writing. I'm outta here.

Wednesday, September 6

My hand is still tired, so this will be short. I'll just keep to the important facts I discovered today:

—*Important fact #1:* The most popular kid in my class is Tyler. Not only is he popular (even with the girls), but he's also really good at spelling, and math, and football, and soccer, and just about everything. His best friend is Zach, who keeps staring at me when he thinks I'm not looking.

—*Important fact #2:* Amy's best friend is named Libby. They are having a contest to see how long they can make their new pencils last.

—*Important fact #3:* Emerson, the guy who gave up his front-row seat for me, eats even more junk food than I do. Today in PE he told me he wants to be an actor when he grows up. I tried to imagine him up on stage or in a movie, but my brain kept saying, "This does *not* compute!"

—*Important fact #4:* Ms. B *loves* Ralph the hamster. She talks to him and calls him Ralphster. She's got his cage inside an old TV cabinet so we can watch "hamster-vision." It only gets one channel, though— the Hamster Channel.

—*REALLY Important fact #5*: I, Cody Lee Carson—as in the one and only New Me—am in the top reading group! First time ever in my entire life.

Who's da man?
I'M da man!

Friday, September 8

Spelling test today—did New Me great.

Multiplication tables pop quiz—oops, Old Me not so great.

But after that I read aloud—did I mention that I'm in the top reading group?—and Ms. B said I read with "expression."

Then she gave the class a writing assignment: "Write about what you did during the summer."

We groaned. At the start of the school year, every kid in the entire universe has to write about what they did during the summer.

Ms. B added, "On a porch."

Yep, a porch. Could be our porch, a friend's porch, Grandma's porch, whatever porch we want. But we have to write a paragraph about what we did, or saw, or heard, or smelled, or thought during the summer, on a porch. It's due in one week.

You want it, Ms. B, you got it. I'm Cody Lee Carson, ace-brilliant-type-author-guy.

Who always did want to write about a porch.

Sunday, September 10

Emma is one smart cat. She doesn't like stale water in her bowl, so she's figured out how to turn on the faucet in the downstairs bathroom. Dad says he'd have no problem with that if she'd just turn the water off when she's done.

Instead of writing about Emma, what I should be doing right now is writing about a porch. Only problem is that it's different when you're writing for a teacher, and a grade. It seems . . . I don't know, just harder, that's all.

Maybe I'll go for a bike ride instead.

Wednesday, September 13

Ms. B brought a fancy electric pencil sharpener to school for us. It's not as noisy as our regular one and lots faster. I stuck my brand-new #2 in there and it almost got eaten alive. (Amy and Libby are still having their short pencil contest. They'd better watch out!)

I told Ms. B we should name her sharpener Godzilla since it has such a big appetite. "Very clever, Cody," Ms. B said, then announced to the class: "From now on the sharpener will be known as Godzilla."

She called me clever, *very* clever. Teachers have called me lots of things, but never that. Very clever is the same as brainy, in case you didn't know. Cody-Lee-New-Me-Very-Clever-Brainy Carson!

Thursday, September 14

Yikes! I just remembered: the porch paragraph is due tomorrow, and I haven't even started!

Later, Thursday, September 14

Whew! Done! And pretty amazing, if I do say so myself. Although bad porch ideas kept popping into my mind, I thought about those state tests we take—you know, where you have to write a descriptive paragraph—and I described watching the sunset from my front porch. This is it:

Oh, the sublimity porch, where I sit prismatic and watch the cadaverous birds roost in the punctilious tree! The crepuscular sun shines through the excrutiation leaves, and casts shadows of conniption at my feet! I redolent, and smile! Oh, the sublimity porch!

Beautiful, huh? That's how Shakespeare and those other dead guys wrote. I used the thesaurus to find the big fancy descriptive words. Then I checked all the spelling, and punctuation, too. I copied the whole thing over onto Mom's stationery and put it in one of those binders with the clear plastic on the front. It looks really halcyon. Ms. B will love it. It's called "A Porch to Remember." I'm bound to get a New Me ace-brilliant-type-author-guy A.

Friday, September 15

Turned in "A Porch to Remember." I wanted Ms. B to read it right then and there, and tell me how great it is, and that it should be published. But she just said, "Thank you," and put it in a pile.

Saturday, September 16

MC invited a kid from her kindergarten class over to play. He has big ears, and wears a Mariners cap that pushes them out even more. His name is Jordy.

It rained for the first time in forever. MC and Jordy jumped up and down in the biggest mud puddle in the neighborhood until they were totally covered with brown ooze. (Jordy even had it in his big ears.)

Sunday, September 17

I keep thinking that I should have a for-real title for this journal, especially since this will be a priceless exhibit in the Cody Lee Carson Museum of Really Great Literature.

Titles are important, you know. When you look at a book on the shelf in the library (like the Benton Library, where my mom works), that's the first thing you see. If the title is interesting, you'll pick the book up. If it's not, then you probably won't. Like if I wrote a book called *Book #1,* you'd pass right on by. So I have to come up with something good.

But I still can't think of a title for this journal. I guess I'll just call it *Put Title Here* for now.

Monday, September 18

Thought I'd get "A Porch to Remember" back today with a big A at the top, but Ms. B's not done grading yet.

I guess she's been too busy thinking—about field trips. Because today after lunch she said, "If we could go anywhere together as a class, where would you like to go?"

Tyler said, "The Grand Canyon."

I liked that idea. I've always wanted to see the Grand Canyon. Ms. B said it was a good idea, but would take too long to get there.

Libby suggested the beach. "Let's go out on the ocean looking for whales!"

"Whales are my favorite animals," Ms. B said, "but I get seasick just washing the dishes."

While I was busy trying to figure out if Ms. B was joking, Amy said that since we'll be studying ecosystems a lot in science this year, maybe it would help us to understand them better if we camped out in the middle of one.

Everybody liked that idea, including Ms. B. All the kids wanted to leave tomorrow, but Ms. B said that a trip like that takes lots of planning *and* money. "We'll need to work really hard to raise enough to go." We all said we would, so Ms. B said okay. And just like that, it was settled. In June we're going on an Incredible-Fantastic-End-of-the-Year Camp-Out! Yahoo!

Tuesday, September 19

Today during U.S. history, Ralphster the hamster tried to climb out of his TV cage and got stuck behind his exercise wheel. He started squealing and going crazy. Amy jumped up and was to the rescue before Ms. B could even get out from behind her desk. After Amy freed him, both she and Ms. B petted the top of his little head and kissed it like he was a real baby, and kept saying, "Are you all right, Ralphster?"

I like Ralphster fine and would give the Hamster Channel pretty high ratings. But I could *never* kiss a rodent.

After we got back to business, Ms. B announced that we, the students of Garfield Elementary, will be picking a fifth grader as the new president of the student council.

"A third grader will serve as secretary," Ms. B said, "a fourth grader as vice president." She swirled her hands around as she talked, like she was painting a wonderful picture for us. "But *only* a fifth grader may be elected president."

I thought, Hmm—Cody Lee Carson, student council president. Has a nice ring to it. . . . But no, I'm too busy being an ace-brilliant-type-author-guy to get into politics.

Speaking of brilliant writing, here's my latest (it's a poem, in case you didn't know):

There once was a guy, the New Me,
who was as popular as can be.
He never goofed up,
or whined like a pup.
Cooler than cool was he!

I'm sure it'll end up in the Cody Lee Carson Museum of Really Great Literature, along with "A Porch to Remember."

Speaking of which, it's *still* not back. I guess Ms. B is waiting to hear which New York publisher is going to turn it into a best-seller.

Wednesday, September 20

In the cafeteria Libby told us she'd read an article in *USA Today* that said that only 21 percent of kids who bring lunch to school pack it themselves. "Moms do 64 percent," she said, "and dads 11 percent. But here's the weird part: 4 percent of kids have no idea who packs their lunch."

Tyler shook his head. "I used to let anybody pack mine, until last year when Aunt Emily put in a liver paté sandwich."

Zach said, "That's nothing. My mom makes me slug sandwiches every day. Anybody want a bite?"

Zach is all the time talking about gross things like slugs and boogers. He'll point and say, "There's a slug on your shoe!" even when there isn't. Or he'll act like he's picking his nose and flicking boogers up on the ceiling. He'll keep looking up there, then pretend the boogers drop on someone's head, like Emerson's. I used to do that kind of stuff when I was the Old Me, but not anymore.

Anyway, back to the cafeteria. Everybody cringed and said things like "Yuck! No!" and "Eeeeuw, gross!"

But Amy didn't bat an eye, not even when Zach shook his sandwich in her face. She just said, "Thanks, I'd love to, but I'm a vegetarian. See?" She picked up three Tater Tots and started juggling them, then caught them—one, two, three—in her mouth!

And all this time I'd been thinking that the only things Amy was good at were school and keeping quiet about seeing me in my . . . you know, my underwear, and making her pencil last a long time. But she's got talent!

Thursday, September 21

I can't believe it, I got a *C* on "A Porch to Remember." Yes, a C, as in "just average." The New Me is not just average. The New Me is an ace-brilliant-type-author-guy who used all those cool words from the thesaurus, and got the spelling right, and the punctuation, too.

At the top of my paper Ms. B wrote, "Don't try to impress me—just write. Find your true voice."

My *true* voice? All my true voice is saying right now is "Ugh!"

Friday, September 22

Worked hard on my math today, to show Ms. B that I'm not just average at that, too. When I handed it in, she said, "For homework I'd like you to seriously consider running for student council president. Answer due on Monday."

Sunday, September 24

Been seriously considering running for student council president. Today I ate breakfast thinking about it. Sat in church thinking about it. Walked into Fred Meyer with Mom and Dad and MC to get some teriyaki sauce thinking about it.

Then, as I was standing in aisle 12, I closed my eyes and imagined the New Me as President Cody. I could be great and accomplish many things for the good of Garfield students. Like a longer morning recess. And chocolate milk shakes in the cafeteria. Or maybe soft drinks in the water fountains. Everyone would love it. And they'd love me, too! And chant my name.

"President Cody! President Cody! President Cody!"

I'd be a superstar!

"President Cody! President Cody! President Cody!"

With lots of friends!

"President Cody! President Cody! President Cody!"

When I opened my eyes, there was MC looking up at me with a cantaloupe in her hands. She said, "Whatever you're thinking about doing, *don't*."

Ha! Since when do I need advice from a five-year-old? Ms. B knows my destiny—that's why she suggested it. I'm going to be an ace-brilliant-type-*politician*-guy! Today Garfield Elementary student council president, tomorrow the White House!

Hear Ye, Hear Ye! Listen Up, Everybody! I, Cody Lee Carson, am going for the top!

Monday, September 25

Well, I did it. I officially nominated myself for Garfield student council president. Only problem is, so did Amy. And Tyler. Not to mention a really smart girl named Kylie in Mrs. Larsen's class.

So all of a sudden I'm thinking of lots of reasons why, on second thought, I *shouldn't* run for student council president:

—Not qualified
—Overqualified
—Really am a kindergartner in disguise
—Really am a senior citizen in disguise
—Doctor told me not to run
—Parents told me not to run
—Sister told me to go ahead and run, and that's a bad sign
—Can't stand failure
—Can't stand success
—My mind is too tense
—My mind is too relaxed
—My mind is missing, and that's a bad sign
—Have to quit to save the world
—Have to quit to go to bed
—Not enough time to prepare election day speech
—Too much time to prepare election day speech
—Can't stop worrying about election day speech, and that's a *really* bad sign!

Tuesday, September 26

Emerson came up to me today in the hall and told me that I shouldn't run for president without a campaign manager. "You know," he said, "a person who helps you get elected. Libby is helping Amy. Zach is helping Tyler. And that girl in Mrs. Larsen's class, Kylie, has someone helping her, too." He smiled. "So I thought you might want to think about having a campaign manager, too—like me!"

"You?" I said. Which was kind of an Old Me thing to do, I guess. But I couldn't help it. Emerson as anything other than Mr. Junk Food is hard for me to imagine.

Emerson's smile dropped straight to the floor. He mumbled, "Okay . . . well, if you don't want me, I guess you could . . . get someone else." He turned and started to slouch away.

That's when I remembered how he gave up his seat for me on the first day of school. And how he is all the time doing nice things for other people, too, like letting Amy and Libby in front of him in line, and giving Zach a Tootsie Roll, even though Zach isn't nice to him and calls him Fat Boy.

And then I thought about how smart Emerson is. And that he probably really could be a big help with the (gulp!) speech I have to make on election day. So I told Emerson he could be my campaign manager.

You'd think I'd told him he'd won a million

dollars. He whirled around with a big ear-to-ear grin on his face. "I'll get you into office, Cody!" he said. "Just leave everything to me!"

Wednesday, September 27

This morning my new campaign manager said, "The first thing we have to do is create a campaign slogan for you. Something that will appeal to the voting public, like 'Friend of the People!' or 'Cody's the One!'"

During math I came up with a list of better suggestions:

1. Don't be toady—vote for Cody!
2. Four out of five doctors recommend Cody—the fifth one's a bozo brain!
3. Vote for Cody—it's easier than thinking!
4. If you carrot all, peas vote for Cody! (Pretty punny, huh?)
5. (My personal favorite.) Don't pick your nose—pick Cody!

Despite how good those were, in the end we decided to keep it simple—"Vote for Cody" with three exclamation marks at the end, which is like shouting—VOTE FOR CODY!!!

Even with all this election stuff, Amy and

Libby are still having a pencil length contest. Their #2s are so short, they have to write with their hands in little fists. Looks uncomfortable to me. But hey, whatever floats your boat.

Saturday, September 30

Emma left the water on again in the bathroom. Dad had to shut it off under the sink.

MC keeps saying it's not her turn to clean out Emma's litter box, whether it is or not. Mom and Dad are no help. They think we need to work it out ourselves. The only problem is that it's getting to be less work to just go ahead and do the job than fight with MC about it. But if I do that, then I get mad, because that's not fair. There's GOT to be a way I can make MC do her share.

Sunday, October 1

Jordy—the little kid with the big ears—came over again. He and MC spent the whole afternoon finding dead bugs and gluing them onto a piece of cardboard.

Emerson called after dinner to tell me I'm behind in the polls, and we'd better come up with a new strategy quick . . . like chocolate. "We could give it away," he said, "along with campaign buttons, to every kid in the school! *That* would get the vote out!"

Chocolate is my favorite food, of course, but I reminded Emerson that chocolate costs money, and that there are over 450 kids at Garfield Elementary School.

Emerson said, "You need to invest in your future." Which was his way of saying that to win I've got to spend big bucks.

I said, "But I've only got thirteen dollars and eighty-five cents. How about we test the chocolate giveaway thing first, to see if it works? On a small group. Of small eaters."

"Kindergartners!" Emerson said. "We'll slip the chocolate to them and a cool 'Vote for Cody!!!' button at lunch. You give them a little speech, and they'll be fighting to vote for you!"

"Speech?" I said. I'd been working hard to forget that word. "I'm not ready yet."

Emerson said, "Sure you are! Just a short—"

"No!"

There was a long silence in which I could hear Emerson let out a long, low sigh. Finally he said, "Okay, no speech tomorrow. We'll just give away the chocolate and—hey, I've got it! You can pull the chocolate and buttons out of a hat so it will look like a magic trick! Voters expect politicians to do magic!"

I said, "But I *can't* do magic."

"I'll teach you!" Emerson said. "No big deal. It's easy!"

Monday, October 2

My dictionary defines *easy* as "requiring little thought or effort."

Notice, however, that there is nothing anywhere in that definition about pulling off the first magic trick of your political career (not to mention your entire life) in front of a bunch of kindergartners in the Garfield cafeteria. Turns out there's a reason: there's nothing easy about it. Especially if your little sister and her friend Jordy are sitting beside each other in the audience.

Before I could even begin to get started, MC held up a french fry and said, "Hey, Cody, you want to see something?"

I ignored her, of course. It says right here in my *Big Brother Instruction Book:* "Ignore little sister whenever possible." I pulled out the magic hat Emerson had given me.

"Something *really* cool?" Now it was Jordy. He grinned as MC carefully laid the french fry on the palm of his right hand. "I've been practicing a lot!"

I ignored Jordy, too. It also says right here in my *Big Brother Instruction Book:* "Same goes for her friends." I held up my magic hat for everyone to see, just like Emerson had taught me.

"Ready-aim-fire!" MC blurted out. Jordy popped his hand up and catapulted the french fry right into his open mouth.

The kindergartners broke into applause. MC and Jordy took this as a sign to go for an encore. "Ready-aim-fire!" Right in the mouth *again*.

"Ready-aim-fire!"

I know this is going to be hard to believe, but I swear that if you saw a slow-motion replay of that third catapulted french fry, you'd see it flip end-over-end as it arched upward and—this is the truly amazing part— go shooting right up Jordy's left nostril.

Everything was quiet for a moment as we all gawked in disbelief. Then kids jumped up, yelling, "Wow! Do that again! Do that again!"

I looked to Emerson for help. This was *not* going according to plan. "Do something!" I said between clenched teeth.

Emerson blinked and muttered, "Uh . . ."

Clearly, he didn't have a clue.

Jordy did, though. He yanked the french fry from his nose and, with great dramatic flair, popped it into his mouth.

"Eeeeuw, yuck!" the kindergartners screamed. But it was Emerson who ended up stealing the show back. He went pale, gagged, then threw up. Yep, threw up—as in puked, hurled, blew lunch, spewed, erupted like a volcano—right there in the cafeteria.

Tuesday, October 3

Emerson apologized about ten billion times today for getting sick. "I'm sorry, Cody," he said over and over again. "I'm really *really* sorry."

To make up for it, he bought a bunch of chocolate with his own money and gave it out on the playground, along with "Vote for Cody!!!" buttons. Several kids came up to me afterward and said they would vote for me for sure, so I guess his idea worked.

Still, I wish he'd give me a little space. Seems like every time I turn around, he's there, looking like he expects something.

Thursday, October 5

Played football today at recess. We lost to Tyler and Zach's team, but I caught one pass.

MC has her first loose tooth. She said, "I closed my eyes and wished really hard over and over for it to happen, and it did!"

I said, "Ha! If wishing was all it took, I'd be a millionaire."

MC said, "Hmph! That just shows what you don't know. It doesn't work on big stuff, just little stuff!"

I rolled my eyes, but later I couldn't help thinking, Why not give it a try? So here goes: I wish I could win the election without giving a speech. I wish I could win the election without giving a speech. I wish I could win the election without giving a speech.

Friday, October 6

First the bad news: Ms. B looked at me funny and said, "Yes, of course you still have to give a speech."

But there's some good news, too. During the math quiz, I got so uptight that I pressed too hard and broke my pencil lead.

You might be thinking: This is good news? Yes! You see, if I hadn't broken my pencil lead, then I wouldn't have walked over to Godzilla to sharpen it. And if I hadn't walked over to Godzilla, then I wouldn't have been right behind Amy while she was sharpening her stubby little pencil. And if I hadn't been right behind Amy, then I wouldn't have been there when Godzilla jerked her stubby little pencil out of her hand.

Amy jumped back, screaming, "It's eating it!" The noise coming from Godzilla was incredible, like rocks in a blender. Ralphster the hamster went wild in his cage, squeaking and going around and around on his exercise wheel. Kids clapped their hands over their ears. Ms. B hustled across the room, saying, "It's okay! It's okay!" Even though the look in her eyes was saying, "No, it's not! No, it's not!"

Tyler jumped up out of his seat and started banging on Godzilla. But the monster wasn't fazed. It kept grinding Amy's pencil into splinters. Things were looking kind of bad . . .

Until—in a very New Me moment—a voice came into my head. It said, "Pull the plug, Cody."

So I pulled the plug. Godzilla made a sound kind of like a burp, then ground to a halt.

Ms. B picked up Godzilla and looked down its throat. "Whew! For a second there I thought it was going to eat the entire classroom. Quick thinking, Cody." She patted me on the back. "Our hero saves the day!"

Which I like the sound of—Cody Lee "Our Hero" Carson.

Later, Amy came up to me and said, "Thanks!"

Which was nice, too . . . I guess.

Saturday, October 7

MC invited that Jordy kid over *again*. Dad says, "They're like two peas in a pod." Meaning they're both trouble.

No kidding. A guy can't get any privacy when they're around. They were playing tag (which Mom had already told them twice not to do in the house) when MC came blasting into my room with Jordy chasing right behind her.

I didn't see or hear them. That's because I was listening to a CD through my head-phones. And I had my eyes closed. And I guess I was sort of dancing to the music and acting like I was playing the guitar, in my . . . I hate to say it . . . in my underwear.

When I finally realized MC and Jordy were there, they were pointing at me and laughing. I yelled at them. "Get lost!" They said, "Oops!" and left. I sure wish they hadn't seen me danc-ing around like that, especially Jordy. What if he's a blabbermouth?

Sunday, October 8

MC's tooth is getting lots looser. She keeps making Dad and Mom wiggle it, but I won't—unless she does her share of cleaning Emma's kitty litter.

Which she hasn't.

Which is a problem.

A BIG problem.

So I started thinking, Sometimes to solve a

BIG problem, you have to do like Ms. B says and "think outside the box." That doesn't mean the kitty litter box. "The box" is just a way of saying how most people see things. So if you "think outside the box," you're hatching new and creative ideas, stuff most people wouldn't dream up.

Might as well give it a try: Think outside the box. Think outside the box. Think outside the box.

Monday, October 9

Ms. B said she couldn't have her students being devoured by a pencil sharpener, so she took Godzilla home. "He's happily perched on my kitchen counter," she said, "where I feed him a pencil every day for breakfast."

Thursday, October 12

Today was school picture day. Lots of kids were really dressed up. Tyler even had on a tie! Zach kidded him about it, saying, "You look like a geek!" I felt sorry for Tyler. When I was the Old Me, I used to get teased a lot. But Tyler didn't seem to mind. He said, "You're just jealous 'cause you're not as handsome." Zach punched him on the arm. Tyler punched Zach back, and they both laughed.

It was nearly lunch by the time our class lined up by height and marched down the hall to get our pictures taken. The photo guy had his stuff set up in a corner of the gym. When it was my turn, he adjusted the stool, then had me sit down just the way he wanted. He went and looked at me through his camera. "Chin up a little, okay?"

I raised my chin.

"No, not that much. Down a little."

I lowered my chin.

"Up just a hair."

I raised my chin a hair.

"Okay," Photo Guy said.

I thought, Whew! Now would you *please* just take the pic—

"Tilt your head to the left," said Photo Guy.

I rolled my eyes, but tilted my head to the left.

"No, not that left." Photo Guy laughed. "The other left."

I tilted my head in the other direction.

"Too far," Photo Guy said.

I tilted my head back a little.

"Great!" Photo Guy said.

"Finally," I muttered.

Photo Guy peered at me through his camera again. "Okay, smile!"

Smile? After all that? I took a deep breath and tried. Zach laughed. "Haw! Look at that cheesy grin!"

I felt myself getting red in the face. I was just about to tell Zach to shut up, when—poof!—bright light exploded in my face as Photo Guy's flash went off. I jumped and almost fell off the stool.

Friday, October 13

After all the Old Me bad luck yesterday getting my picture taken, I figured today would be a New Me piece of cake, Friday the thirteenth or not. Until lunch, that is. MC and Jordy were coming out of the cafeteria as my class was going in. When she saw me, MC said, "Look, Cody, my tooth fell out!" She opened really wide. "I've got a window in my mouth!"

Jordy bounced up and down beside her. "I've got a window, too! See?"

From behind me in line Amy said, "I see, Jordy. That's nice!"

After MC and Jordy went skipping off, I asked Amy, "How do you know Jordy?"

She gave me a puzzled look. "He's my brother."

"Right," I said, like of course I knew that, just forgot for a second, that's all. But inside I was thinking, Yikes! Jordy's been over at my house a gazillion times, and it never once entered my mind to ask about his family. He was just my pesky little sister's pesky little friend, someone to be ignored. Until he came blasting into my room and saw me dancing around in my . . . underwear! I really really really don't want Amy to know about that. That would be really really really embarrassing!

Really.

Hoping for some New Me good luck, I said, "Molly and I don't get along very well. We don't talk much. Probably the same with you and Jordy, huh?"

Amy smiled. "No, we get along fine. Talk a lot, too. Jordy tells me *everything*."

Friday the thirteenth. It'll get you every time.

Sunday, October 15

Gotta get rolling on my election speech. Gotta get that ace-brilliant-type-author-guy feeling again. Gotta find my "true voice," like Ms. B said.

Yep. Gotta.

Only problem is that every time I even think about it, my stomach does an Old Me nosedive to my toes. Think I'll go watch one of the old *Star Wars* movies, instead. Love that sci-fi!

Thursday, October 19

"Hey, Cody, guess what?" Emerson said to me today at recess. He held up a football. "My dad says I'd make a good center, so I've been practicing snapping the ball. I'm getting good. Watch this!"

"Watch this"? Didn't he know? Say those famous last words and something is bound to go wrong.

Sure enough. Emerson grinned and put on his best football announcer's voice: "It's fourth and six. Oregon State has the ball on their own thirty yard line." He motioned me to get behind him. "Carson is back to punt." He spread his legs wide and scowled like he was one mean dude on the football field.

"Down! Set!" Emerson yelled, then bent over really fast, just like they do at the beginning of a play. There was a loud ripping sound. Lucky me. I had a perfect view of the seat of Emerson's pants splitting wide open.

Emerson jumped up and slapped his hand over the rip. "Oh no!" He looked around the playground to see if anyone besides me had noticed. Some first graders had stopped playing tag and were looking his way. One of them giggled. "What do I do?" Emerson begged. "Help me, Cody!"

I have to admit that my first thought was an Old Me thought: make myself scarce as fast as possible. Don't be seen anywhere even close to a guy whose underwear is trying to escape.

But then I remembered my fourth-grade play, and I felt sorry for Emerson. So I did the New Me thing: I gave him my jacket to wrap around his waist and hustled him into the building.

No sooner had we gotten inside, though, than there came Zach down the hall. "Quick!" I said. "In here!" I jerked open the nearest door and ducked in, pulling Emerson behind me.

"But Cody!" Emerson said. "This is—"

"Quiet!" I said, my ear to the door. "He'll hear us!"

"But Cody!" Emerson insisted.

"SHHH!" I hissed over my shoulder. "Believe me, you *don't* want Zach to see you like this!" Not to mention that I didn't want Zach to see *me* like that.

The sound of footsteps grew near, then went past. I eased open the door and peered out. No one in sight. "Whew!" I whispered. "All clear!"

"Not exactly," came a voice from behind us.

Emerson and I both jumped and whirled around to see Amy standing there. *There* being the middle of the girls' bathroom, which BOZO DUFUS ME had ducked us into.

Emerson gasped and slapped his hands over the rip in his pants. Amy's eyebrows went up and a little smile snuck onto the corners of her mouth. I moaned and waited for the laughter. "Haw! Haw!" she'd say, finally letting it all out. "First I saw you in the dressing room at Mattingly's. Then Jordy told me about you dancing in your bedroom. And now your friend's underwear has escaped. Wait until I tell everybody. Haw! Haw!"

But the only thing Amy said was, "Emerson, you've got a problem."

Emerson tried to speak, but all that came out was a little squeak.

"Don't worry—I can help," Amy said, "but first we need to move." And with that, she was hustling us out of the girls' bathroom and next door into the janitor's closet. "Wait here," she said. "I've still got a needle and thread in my desk from the little quilt I made for my history project. Emerson, you can stitch your pants back up in no time!"

Emerson started to protest. "But, Amy—"

She waved him off. "Be back in a flash!"

Emerson looked around at all the mops and buckets and brooms. "But, Cody," he said, "I can't sew."

Guess who ended up doing the repair work while Amy guarded the janitor's closet door? Yep, good ol' New Me. I'm not too bad with a needle and thread, if I do say so myself.

So today I became Cody Lee "Our Hero" Carson for the second time in two weeks! Cool, huh?

Monday, October 23

During math Ralphster tried to escape again, this time by climbing up on the shoe-box house Amy had put in his TV cage. He was halfway out when Emerson happened to spot him.

Emerson nudged me (I was working on my division, like a good political candidate), and pointed and said, "Get him!" So I did, and I was a hero *again*. Which is very presidential, in case you didn't know. Lots of presidents were heroes first. Anyway, Amy thanked me at least ten times, and Ms. B even gave me a hug!

Saturday, October 28

Today was MC's birthday, so we had to have a party. She invited four of her friends—Jordy included, of course—for hot dogs and potato chips and cake. They drank lots of pop, too, and had a burping contest.

Just to make conversation, I asked Jordy how Amy was doing. MC giggled and said, "Cody *loves* Amy!" For a second I gave some serious Old Me thought to smacking her. But then I just let it go. I'm mature. Anyway, I don't love Amy. She's just a friend, that's all.

Sunday, October 29

Carved pumpkins after dinner, then posed with them for a photo. Mom's is especially cool. She calls it Frankenkitty.

Every year I come up with a Halloween plan for scaring trick-or-treaters. Last year in Portland I cut a hole in an old sheet stained with ketchup. I put the sheet over my head, then put on a gross-out mask and sat in Dad's rolling office chair in a dark corner of our front porch. When a little girl came to trick-or-treat, I gave myself a push and rolled out at her, shrieking at the top of my lungs.

Which may sound pretty cool, and it was. I scared her so bad she wet her pants. Only problem is her big brother was out on the front sidewalk, and came charging to his little sister's rescue. Scared me so bad I ended up wetting *my* pants.

Old Me stuff. Yep.

This year, though, is going to be different . . . if I can just think of a trick.

A really good trick.

That can't backfire.

You see, Amy said she's going to come trick-or-treating at my house.

Monday, October 30

Racked my brain all morning to come up with a Halloween trick for our front porch. Was about to give up. But then in PE we ran laps around the playground, and I was flying along in front of everybody (I'm pretty fast), not thinking about anything in particular and—*pop!*—into my mind came a perfect idea. This is it—the Gotcha Box!

trick-or-treater (ghost)

stiff paper flaps

small box for candy

hole in top of box

Cody inside Gotcha Box, waiting to grab trick-or-treaters when they reach for candy

the Gotcha Box

Mom said, "It's a work of pure and stagger-ing genius!" and took me to the appliance store to get a big box.

Tuesday, October 31

All I could think about at school today was get-ting home to start Halloween. Finally it got dark and I put on my pirate costume (complete with a patch over one eye, fake blood on my face, and a wooden sword), then I lit candles in the jack-o'-lanterns and squeezed into the Gotcha Box. MC (who decided to be my elf assistant) told the first trick-or-treater that showed up (a ghost) to help himself. "Take as much as you want," she said.

The kid started to haul in a big bunch of candy and—GOTCHA!—I reached up and grabbed him. He let out a big scream and jumped back so fast he almost fell down. Then he laughed and said, "Cool!" Pretty soon bunches of kids were showing up. GOTCHA! GOTCHA! I had them screaming all over the place.

As fun as that was, though, after a while I was ready to load up on goodies for *me*. But as I was crawling out from under the Gotcha

Box, I heard some familiar voices coming up the sidewalk—Amy and Libby and Jordy—so I hustled back just in time.

"Where's Cody?" Amy asked MC, coming up onto the porch.

MC covered for me. "Oh, he had to go fix his costume."

Amy bought it, but was still suspicious, I could tell. She watched Jordy take some candy. I did nothing. Then Libby took some. Again I did nothing. So Amy thought it was all right. She reached for the goodies and I grabbed her wrist and almost pulled her right in. She shrieked so loud I thought someone would call 911.

"Gotcha!" I said, coming out from under the box.

"Cody!" she said, acting like she was mad. But then she laughed. She was dressed as the Wicked Witch of the West from *The Wizard of Oz*. She had a pointy black hat and a broom, and cool striped socks with a hidden button that said "Boo!" when she pressed it.

Libby was dressed as a cafeteria worker, complete with green apron and plastic gloves and a hair net. On a tray she had all sorts of rotten food and fake flies. She kept saying, "Be sure to take some of the creamed corn," just like they do at school. It was creepy.

Jordy had a bunch of car parts duct-taped to him. "I'm an engine!" he explained. "Watch! I'll start!" He turned his eyelids inside out and said, "Varoom! Scary, huh?" Amy rolled her eyes, and I knew she was thinking the same thing as me: No, just weird.

MC and Jordy started whispering and giggling about me being in love with Amy—WHICH I AM NOT!—so I came after them with a jack-o'-lantern. They just giggled some more.

After they left, it was time to get some sugar for me. I started down the steps when two vampires walked around the corner—Tyler and Zach. So I ducked into the Gotcha Box again and got Tyler good. He liked the box even more than Amy. "Awesome!" he said. "Can I try it?" Zach said, "Me too!" We ended up having a great time taking turns, and I was thinking, Maybe I could be Tyler and Zach's friend.

But then four sixth-grade boys showed up: Whit, Nate, Deshawn, and Theo. I'd seen them before, playing basketball after school at the park. And all of a sudden Zach said my Gotcha Box was for little kids, and they should get out of there and pull some *real* tricks. The next thing I knew, all the guys were gone, and they hadn't invited me, or even said thanks.

I *really* needed some chocolate by then. I'd

started down the steps when Dad called, "Nine o'clock, Cody. School night. Remember our agreement?" So I had to go to bed and ended up with only a few pieces of leftover candy corn.

Halloween! Who needs it?

Thursday, November 2

Slept lousy last night. Kept waking up thinking about my speech. Which I still haven't started. And parent conferences. Which are tomorrow. Ms. B will tell Mom and Dad about my C in writing. And those times tables tests I can't seem to pass.

What, me worried?

YES, ME WORRIED! It'll look like I'm still the Old Me—bad-grade city—when really the New Me is trying SUPER hard to do the right thing.

A new poem:

> Rain.
> All day long.
> Gloom.
> Doom.
> Lock me in my room.

Friday, November 3

"Let me begin by telling you how glad I am to have Cody in my class this year!"

That's the first thing Ms. B said to Mom and Dad today at my conference.

I sat there with my mouth hanging open, like I hadn't heard right. But I had.

Ms. B laughed and said, "You have a wonderful son, Mr. Carson." Then she went on to tell him and Mom how well I was doing in school. Sure, I still needed to work on my times tables. And yes, my writing could improve. (Haven't found my "true voice" yet is what she meant.) But I was doing great in reading. And I'd aced the science test, and done really well on my history project. And she was *so* proud that I was running for student council president, and on and on and on . . .

Dad patted me on the shoulder, and Mom was so happy, she hugged me right there in front of Ms. B. It was embarrassing, but not really. The New Me was paying off. My parents were proud of me!

So proud we went out for pizza and then for a chocolate sundae at Ice Cream Hill. And I thought, It doesn't get much better than this.

But it did. When we got home there was a message on the answering machine from Amy. She wished me good luck on Tuesday. She said, "You'll do great on the speech, Cody!" And I found myself thinking, Things are really looking up. I should call this journal *The Rise of Cody Lee Carson*.

Sunday, November 5

Worked all day on my speech.

Did so much writing, my hand feels like it's going to fall off.

But I think it's pretty good.

So does Emerson.

I called him up and read it to him.

After practicing in front of the mirror.

You're probably wondering why I'm writing like this, huh?

One-liners?

I have no idea.

My brain is fried.

I'm going to bed.

Good night!

Monday, November 6

Finished my speech. It's called "Why I Should Be in Charge of the World." Listed all the things I'd do if elected. You know, stuff we really need:

1. Longer recesses
2. Housecleaning machines
3. Four days of Christmas
4. Milk shakes on Fridays
5. Red cars that don't dent
6. Baby-sitters that let you go to your room

Also, I listed the things we *don't* need:

1. Liver for dinner
2. Snotty sisters
3. Blisters from new shoes
4. Boring Mondays
5. Doctor appointments
6. Fences around yards
7. Kitty litter boxes (*especially* kitty litter boxes)
8. Parents ruling kids all the time

Cool writing, huh? I'm *bound* to get elected!

Tuesday, November 7
Election Day

According to Mom's almanac, the ten worst human fears are (going from bad to worse):

10. Dogs
9. Loneliness
8. Flying
7. Death
6. Sickness
5. Deep water
4. Financial problems
3. Insects and bugs
2. Heights

Guess what number one is.
Speaking in front of a group.
Guess why.
Because it's scarier than all of the other nine put together—that's why! And I'm never going to do it again, ever, much less show my face at Garfield Elementary! Is that clear?

Maybe I should explain. The day started out fine. I got up feeling great. But then on the way to school, MC leaned over in the backseat and said, "Don't do anything weird like you usually do, okay? I'm your sister. It's embarrassing."

I told her not to worry, but started to worry myself. What if I got a fit of Old Me, and my mind went blank in the middle of my speech? Or what if my mind was working, but the kids thought I was boring? What if my tongue got tied and I stumbled over my words? What if my knees started knocking so loud I couldn't think? What if all the work I'd put into my speech was for nothing? What if my pants fell down onstage, like in the fourth-grade play? What if everybody saw me in my underwear? What if they all laughed at me? What if . . . You get the picture.

By the time I got backstage in the auditorium, my mouth was dry, my palms clammy, my pits sweaty. They could have made a deodorant ad about me: "THIS KID NEEDS RIGHT GUARD!" I sat there with Emerson and listened to Tyler give his speech. It was great. Everybody clapped. Then Amy gave her speech, and it was great, too. Kylie, from Mrs. Larsen's room, went on, and Amy came backstage. "Good luck!" she said.

Luck? I didn't need luck. I needed to be rescued! Amy could see the panic in my eyes, I guess. "Here," she said, pulling up a chair. "Sit and take a few deep breaths. It'll calm you down."

Libby, who was standing nearby, said, "Probably not. He's scared."

"I'm not scared!" I lied. "I'm not scared of anything!"

"Everybody," Libby said, her eyes boring into mine, "is afraid of something!"

Which, of course, did nothing to help poor little Old Me. "Maybe they won't notice if I don't give my speech," I whimpered, standing to go. "I could just make a quiet exit and—"

"Sit," Amy said. She gently pushed me back down into the chair. "Breathe slowly and deeply. I read somewhere that that helps. They'll love your speech, Cody. Relax. Drink some water. Emerson, get him some water."

Emerson hustled off the stage. He was back in ten seconds with a cup in hand. "Here, Cody! Fresh from the water fountain, brought to you by—*whoa!*"

You know how in movies sometimes they'll switch to slow motion so you can see everything clearly? That's what the next split second was like for me. Clearly, I saw Emerson stumble over his own feet. Clearly, I saw the cup fly from his hand. Clearly, I saw it coming right at me. Clearly, I saw it all, but could do absolutely nothing to stop it, since I was in s-l-o-w m-o-t-i-o-n, too.

Then that cold water hit my lap and everything went from slow motion to hyperspeed. I jumped up. "Oh no!" It looked like I'd wet my pants.

Emerson freaked. "I didn't mean to, Cody! Really I didn't! Quick, come with me!" He grabbed me by the arm and pulled me out the backstage door and across the hall into the boys' bathroom. He jerked paper towels from the dispenser and I wiped and wiped at the spill. It didn't help. It had soaked in!

Emerson paced the bathroom floor. Then an idea hit. "I know!" he said. "Pull out your shirttail and cover up the water!"

Desperate for anything, I pulled out my shirttail, but the water still showed.

Emerson walked around and around in tight little circles, concentrating. Then he grinned. "Got it! Put your pants on backward!"

I stared at him. "*What? No way am I going to—*"

"It'll work!" Emerson said. "Turn them around and then just walk out sideways. Like this!" He demonstrated, shuffling sideways across the bathroom floor. "See? Nobody will notice. Really!"

From the gym I could hear our beloved principal, Mrs. Mead, announcing the next speaker—me. I closed my eyes and tried to imagine crab-walking onto the stage with my pants on backward.

No way.

So I did what any kid who's shuffling with a full deck would do—I ran. Out of school and all the way home. Where I am going to stay for the rest of my life.

Wednesday, November 8

Hear Ye, Hear Ye! Listen Up, Everybody!

Remember all that stuff I wrote on the first page of this journal about the New Me? Well, forget it. There is no such thing. I thought I'd escaped and started over, that I'd left that old doofus, bozo-brained part of myself behind in Portland. But the truth is that no matter how far I run, I can't hide from the Old Me. My New Life is history, ruined.

Which is enough to make a guy sick.

Which is exactly what I told Mom and Dad this morning: "I can't go to school. I'm sick." Mom put her hand on my forehead and said I didn't feel feverish. But she let me stay home anyway. So now I get to sit here on the couch in my pajamas all day and watch the rain pour down while I go over and over this fact: I was an airhead for thinking I should get into politics. I blew it, and probably lost the election by a gazillion votes. I should call this journal *The Rise and Fall of Cody Lee Carson.*

Or maybe I should just toss it in the garbage.

Yep, that's what I'm going to do, heave it into the stinky trash where it belongs, along with the broken eggshells, and soggy tea bags, and greasy globs of refried beans. So that makes this . . .

THE END

Later, Wednesday, November 8

Okay, okay, so I didn't toss my journal. I tried, but it didn't work. Just as I was standing over the kitchen garbage can with it dangling between two fingers, and I was counting down from ten to the end, there was a knock at the front door. So I tossed it onto the counter and went and opened the door, and there stood Amy.

My face must have gone really pale at the sight of her, because she said, "Boy, you *do* look sick."

I faked a cough. "Yeah. Must be the flu or something." I slunk behind the door and started to close it. "Gotta get back to bed."

"Too bad," Amy said. "I thought you were just embarrassed about what happened yesterday. But if you're really sick, then these wouldn't help, anyway." She smiled and pulled a plate of cookies from behind her back.

Chocolate chip cookies. *Chunky* chocolate chip cookies. *Homemade* chunky chocolate chip cookies.

"Uh. . . ," I said, trying to keep from drooling. "Maybe just one wouldn't hurt."

So anyway, Amy came on in and WOW, were those cookies ever good! She told me that, yes, I had lost the election, but so had she, and Tyler. Kylie from Mrs. Larsen's class had won.

"Oh, well," Amy said with a laugh, "that's life!"

I laughed, too—which actually helped a lot—and ended up eating every one of those cookies—which helped a lot more. "Think of them as flu medicine," Amy said with a wink, and put her hand on my arm for just a second. When she lifted it back up, I could still feel the warmth on my skin. Made my head tingle. In an okay way. I guess.

Thursday, November 9

Going back to school today was hard. Even though Amy said not to worry, I couldn't help it. I kept imagining kids pointing and shouting, "Haw! Haw! It's Chicken-Cody-Runs-Away! Haw! Haw!"

But get this: the weird thing is that not one person teased me—not even Zach!—or even mentioned what had happened. (Except for Emerson, who fell all over himself apologizing for spilling the water.)

Now don't get me wrong. It's not like I wanted to be embarrassed in front of everyone. I've had enough of that Old Me kind of stuff to last a lifetime. Still, kids will be kids, you know. All that politeness seemed downright unnatural!

You may have heard the expression "Don't look a gift horse in the mouth." Which is another way of saying, If something good comes your way, don't be picky—grab it! Well, I don't know for sure who led the gift horse my way, but I've got a sneaking suspicion her name might begin with A-m-y.

Friday, November 10

Still no teasing from anybody at school about election day. I guess it really is water under the bridge. Whew! Things are looking good.

Better than good, actually. I was playing basketball at lunch recess, and the game was tied. Just as the bell started to ring for us to go in, I tossed up a shot—I mean just threw it, hardly looking—and it went in! Swished! All the guys on my team started whooping and shouting. Tyler came up and gave me a high five and said, "All right! Nice shot!"

Saturday, November 11

Jordy was over again to play with MC. They rode down the stairs in a cardboard box, yelling, "Bump! Bump! Bump!" until Dad made them stop. So they stood on their heads until their ears turned red.

Jordy told me about his cousin Rainy, who is eight years old. Rainy bugged his sister so much she slugged him, but then she got into trouble and had to take out the garbage for a month.

Hmm. Not a bad idea, when you think about it. It would be worth getting slugged *ten* times by MC if for punishment she had to clean out the litter box for a month!

Later, Saturday, November 11

Started bugging MC to see if she'd hit me. So far, no luck.

Monday, November 13

New spelling list at school today. One of the words is *poinsettia*. Which is the kind of potted flower you see a lot of around Christmastime. Turns out we're going to sell them to make money for our Incredible-Fantastic-End-of-the-Year Camp-Out.

Ms. B says there's a good "profit margin" on poinsettias, which I think means we make lots of bucks off each one we sell.

Amy wanted to know if she had to sell Christmas flowers since she's Jewish. Ms. B said she'd already thought about that. One of the other spelling words this week is *Hanukkah*. Which, according to Amy and Ms. B, is the Jewish festival of lights. We're going to be selling Hanukkah candles, too!

Wednesday, November 15

Really thought I had MC. I was in the family room bugging her about listening to Elvis Presley, when she hissed at me, "Shut up!" I said, "Make me." She started walking toward me with that look in her eye and I figured, This is it! She's going to slug me, and I'll fall on the floor screaming, and she'll get into so much trouble she'll have to do the litter box for TWO months! I stuck out my tongue at her and said, "Elvis sucks!" just to make sure she was mad enough to do the deed. Then a voice came from the doorway.

Dad's voice. "I happen to like Elvis."

Guess who has to clean out the litter box every day until Christmas? Me! Argh!

Thursday, November 16

Turns out we can't sell poinsettias and Hanukkah candles, after all. Ms. B found out it's against school district policy. So we're going to sell chocolate bars instead. Which is okay with me. Chocolate bars are a product I really believe in!

Monday, November 20

Amy's been spending lots of time watching the Hamster Channel lately. Seems like whenever I look up, she's finished the assignment we're on and is over there by Ralphster's TV home.

Ms. B lets her take him out and play with him sometimes. This afternoon Amy let him crawl up her sleeve. I guess it tickled, because she started to giggle. Ms. B giggled, too, but made Amy put Ralphster back.

Tuesday, November 21

At lunch today I walked past the table where Libby and Amy and a bunch of girls were sitting. I overheard one girl ask the others, "If you *had* to go out with a boy, who would you go out with?" I slowed down and listened for answers, but they all started laughing and talking at once, and I couldn't pick out what any one person said. Like Amy.

Not that I care. I was just curious.

Ms. B drew Libby's name out of a hat, so she gets to take Ralphster home for Thanksgiving. Amy looked disappointed, but then Libby told her she could come visit anytime she wanted. Amy smiled from ear to ear.

Thursday, November 23
Thanksgiving Day

Had turkey for dinner, of course. Dad asked me to carve it. "Nice job, Cody!" he kept saying, even though my slices weren't as neat as his.

For dessert we had pumpkin *and* pecan pie, which Mom got at the Benton Bakery. She could have gotten them cheaper at Wal-Mart, but said, "I buy local!" For a sequel to dessert we had some of my fund-raiser chocolate bars. Mom and Dad paid for them. Ace-brilliant-type-fund-raiser-guy-Me was thankful.

Friday, November 24

MC says it's never okay to kiss a boy. "They always slobber all over you." I asked her how she knew about kissing. She said, "Ken and Barbie kiss all the time! Do you and Amy?"

I said, "I'll tell you if you clean out the litter box."

She said, "I don't want to know that bad!"

Tuesday, November 28

Today at recess a kid named Andrew kept hassling a girl named Amanda. He called her "nugget head," and took the soccer ball away from her, and bumped into her—the same kind of Old Me stuff I used to do in fourth grade to Tiffany in Portland.

Libby says it's a stupid way to show somebody you care. Amy says it's immature. I agree.

Saturday, December 2

MC said I should call this journal *Girls Don't Get Cooties*.

I said, "Mind your own business. I don't need your help to figure out a title." (Even though I haven't yet.)

She covered her ears and said, "I can't hear you!"

I said, "Besides, girls do get cooties. There's one on you right now!"

Ha! You should have seen her run to check in the mirror. Serves her right since I have to do Emma's litter box until Christmas.

Monday, December 4

Today Ms. B said, "We aren't going to have regular math."

Somebody said what I was thinking: "Yippee!"

Ms. B smiled. "We're going to do surveys instead."

We all just kind of sat there until Zach said, "Surveys? You mean like when you ask people questions?"

Ms. B said, "No, not *like* when you ask people questions. We actually are going to *do* the real thing!"

Zach rolled his eyes. He hates it when Ms. B gets on him for saying "like."

But here's the deal: all we have to do is pick a topic and come up with some questions, then go around asking them and write down what people say. Simple!

Maybe. Ms. B says we have to "present the survey findings mathematically," which I think means in a graph or something.

Anyway, I'll worry about that part later.

Right now I'm going to make a list of things I'd like to ask people. Because I always did like to, like, you know, ask lots of, like, questions. Like, How many times a day do you, like, say "like"? (Like, I'm not really, like, going to, like, ask that, though.)

Tuesday, December 5

I got a bunch of survey ideas, and I'm going to do them all! If I can't get an A for quality, I'll get one with tons of New Me quantity! An A for effort if nothing else.

Here's my first topic: food. Everybody has something to say about food.

Here are my questions (and how I'd answer them):

—What's your favorite food? (Chocolate for me, or pizza)
—Least favorite? (Cooked cauliflower)
—How often do you snack? (As often as possible)
—What's the weirdest food you ever ate? (Frog legs, no lie)
—What's the best food to have in a food fight? (Mashed potatoes)

Varoom! I'm off and running! Look! It's a bird! It's a plane! No, it's ace-brilliant-type-Question-Man!

Wednesday, December 6

Got a lot of great answers to my food survey. The grossest was Zach's. He said that when he was at his grandma's house in Kentucky last summer, she made him eat boiled okra. I'd never even heard of okra before, but Zach said, "It's all slimy in your mouth, like snot." I wondered how he knew what snot is like in your mouth, but you don't ask Zach things like that.

Maybe I'll do my next survey on boogers. I could ask how often people pick their nose. And why they do it. And which finger they use. Index? Pinky? And what they do with it afterward. Then again, maybe I won't.

Got 100 on my history test. I may not know a lot about boogers, but anything you want to learn about the Civil War, just ask!

Thursday, December 7

Another cool survey idea from ace-brilliant-type-Question-Man: growing up, as in . . .

   —What do you want to be when you grow up? (A pro basketball player)
   —Are you looking forward to growing up? (Yeah! Then I can drive a car! And eat dessert first.)
   —How do you know when you're grown up? (No more pimples, I'd say. And no one tells you what to do.)

Friday, December 8

Today at recess Libby drew a button on the back of each finger. She made a fist and went around asking the girls in our class to pick a button and push it. When they did, she'd unfold that finger and there was the name of the boy they'd marry. When Libby got to Amy, all the girls started hooting really loud. Amy looked embarrassed.

I wonder which boys Libby had written on her fingers.

By the way, Amy wants to be a veterinarian when she grows up. Libby, a lawyer. Tyler, a teacher. Zach, a race car driver, "or a squirrel poop inspector." Emerson—big surprise here!—an actor.

Saturday, December 9

Great weather today. No rain. Sun even came out and dried up the sidewalk.

Which MC and Jordy figured was in need of decoration. They got colored chalk and were out there all afternoon, which made for peace and quiet inside. It wasn't until I headed over to the park to shoot some hoops that I saw what they'd been doing. In big block letters, stretching from our house to the corner, were the words *CODY LOVES AMY!!!*

I chased them around the house three times, but they kept slipping into the bushes and squirming away. Little worms! In the end I had to get the garden hose out of the garage and hook it back up, then turn the nozzle on full blast to wipe out what they kept calling their "art." Even then you could still see it, though.

For once I'll be really glad when it starts raining again.

Getting REALLY tired of cleaning out Emma's litter box. I asked Dad if he would shorten my punishment. He just laughed.

Monday, December 11

I was in such a hurry to catch a ride to school with Mom this morning that I almost ran out of the house *in my underwear!* After all I've been through, you'd think I'd be more New Me careful.

Thankfully, I caught the Old Me foul-up before I got out the door. Still, it was scary that I could be that much of a space cadet.

Earth to Cody! Earth to Cody! *PAY ATTENTION!*

Tuesday, December 12

During math I looked up and Amy was smiling at me. Just smiling that big pretty smile she has. I smiled back. And for a second we just sat there smiling at each other.

Emerson giggled. I glared at him and whispered, "Lay off it! We're just friends."

New survey topic from ace-brilliant-type-Question-Man: friends, as in, How do you know if a person is more than a friend?

Just wondering.

Wednesday, December 13

Wendell is the custodian at Garfield Elementary School. He's a really nice guy, and does lots of things for kids, like when he helped me fix a flat tire on my bike. He always wears jeans and a plaid shirt and a baseball cap. Ms. B suggested we have a Dress Like Wendell Day. We all said, "Yeah!" Wendell doesn't know, though. It's a surprise!

Thursday, December 14

Somehow Wendell found out about Dress Like Wendell Day. We showed up dressed like him. He showed up dressed in a tuxedo. Ms. B laughed so hard I thought she was going to fall over. Wendell said, "Thank you very much," and gave her a Tootsie Roll. I started laughing really hard, too, but he just patted me on the head.

Friday, December 15

You've probably heard people say that there are times when you feel like you're stuck between a rock and a hard place, meaning that no matter what you do, somebody is going to see it as wrong. That's what happened to me today at recess.

I was playing basketball. Tyler and Zach and I were on the same team. We were doing great, blowing out those boys from Mrs. Larsen's room. I scored. We ran back down the court, and there were Amy and Libby.

At first I thought they had come to watch super-hoop-star Cody, and would break into cheers. But instead of asking me how it is that I got to be so great, Libby said, "We want to play."

Zach frowned and said, "No way."

Amy frowned right back. "Why not?"

"Because you're girls," Zach said, "and girls can't shoot."

I groaned. If I've learned anything about Amy, it's that you *never* tell her she can't do something because she's a girl. Her eyes narrowed. "I'll shoot against you any day, Zach!"

Zach laughed. "In your dreams." He waved her off. "We got a good game going. Go play on the bars or something."

Amy looked at me like I was supposed to do something. Do what? Tell Zach he's being a macho jerk? Well, even if he was, I couldn't do that. And anyway, we already *had* chosen sides. And we *did* have a good game going. And Amy and Libby *could* go do something else. There I stood, between a rock (that would be Amy) and a hard place (Zach), not knowing what to do or say.

Tyler, however, didn't bat an eye. "This isn't the NBA," he said. "They can play." He motioned the girls onto the court. "C'mon. We'll take Amy. Libby, you go to the other side."

I thought Zach was going to argue, for sure. But he just rolled his eyes and said, "Okay," and the next thing I knew we'd gone coed.

Well, sort of. Amy and Libby did start running up and down the court guarding people on defense. And on offense they moved around trying to get open and waved their arms so somebody would pass to them, too. Only problem was, nobody did. I tried to get the ball to Amy once, but Zach cut it off and drove for the basket.

Amy got redder and redder in the face, until finally she threw up her hands and said, "BOYS!" then stomped off the court. When I started to go after her, Zach said, "Let her be!" Libby looked daggers at all of us, but particularly me. "Jerks!" she said, then marched after Amy.

I know I should have said more. I know I should have gone after Amy and Libby, no matter what Zach said. But he threw me the ball and said, "C'mon, let's play!" And that's what I did—play.

For the rest of the day, neither Amy nor Libby would even look at me, much less speak. Every now and then Libby would act like she was coughing and say, "Jerk!" under her breath. Looks like I've gone from between a rock and a hard place to the Old Me doghouse.

Saturday, December 16

Woke up this morning thinking about Amy being mad at me. Headed for the shower. It's a good place to solve problems. Ideas come raining down on my brain along with all that hot water. I'd have this figured out in no time.

But MC was headed for the shower, too. As bad luck would have it, we got to the bathroom door at exactly the same time.

MC said, "I get the shower first."

I said, "No, I do."

"But I stink!"

"I stink worse!"

"No, I do!"

"No, I do!"

"NO, I DO!"

Mom called from the bottom of the stairs: "What's going on up there?"

It was useless. I said to MC, "Okay, you're right. You stink."

MC glared at me. "Mom, Cody said I stink!"

Like I said, useless.

So now I'm back in bed, leaning against my pillow while MC takes her shower. By the time I get in there, all the good ideas will be gone, along with the hot water. Which is why I still haven't figured out how to get on Amy's good side again.

New ace-brilliant-type-Question-Man survey topic: little sisters. Just two questions:

—Do you have one?

—How many times a day do you consider locking her in a closet for the rest of her life?

Sunday, December 17

Got our Christmas tree this afternoon. Cut it at one of the Christmas tree farms outside of town. It's a nice one, taller than Dad.

When we got it home, Mom put on Christmas music and we pulled all the decorations out of the attic. It took at least an hour to get the lights untangled and strung. And at least that much more to hang all the ornaments. By the time we finished, it was almost dark outside. We turned off all the lights in the living room and then plugged in the tree.

"It's so pretty!" MC said, jumping up and down.

Mom put her hand to her mouth. "Absolutely beautiful!"

"Our best tree *ever,*" Dad said, just like he says every year.

I was about to agree with Dad—that's what I do every year—when I noticed Emma crouched on the back of the armchair with a weird look in her eye. "Emma, no!" I yelled.

But it was too late. She'd already attacked. Attacked the Christmas tree. Which went crashing over onto the floor.

Dad cussed. Mom cried. MC said, "Why do we have a cat, anyway?" So now I have *another* ace-brilliant-type-Question-Man survey topic: cats. My questions:

—Why do people have cats, anyway?
—What's the most irritating thing your cat has ever done? (Besides knocking over your Christmas tree. That's already taken.)

Monday, December 18

Tried an experiment today. I was wondering if chocolate can increase brainpower. So I bought a chocolate bar from myself. Then I ate it, and just like that, I knew what to get Amy for Christmas. I could buy her the rest of the chocolate bars (four, I think). That would be a really cool gift.

So there you have it! My conclusion: People think better after eating chocolate. Am I a genius, or what?

And I did it without a shower.

Later, Monday, December 18

What was I thinking? A Christmas present? Amy is Jewish!

Tuesday, December 19

Today at recess a kid in third grade kissed a girl on the playground because someone bet him a dollar he wouldn't. Our beloved principal, Mrs. Mead, found out and made him give the money back. Then she got on the intercom and said, "There is to be *no* kissing for money."

Zach faked like he was really disappointed. "Aw, gee!" he said. "Just when I was feeling all lovey!" He puckered up and acted like he was blowing kisses everywhere. When Libby said, "Gag!" Emerson laughed. For a second I thought Zach was going to punch them both. I mean *really* punch them.

Obviously, kissing is an emotional issue.

New ace-brilliant-type-Question-Man survey topic: kissing.

Questions:

—Who would you most like to kiss?

On second thought, this is not a good survey topic. I'd better come up with something else. Still time enough for one more before they're due on Friday. Boy, is Ms. B gonna be surprised at all the ace-brilliant-type-Question-Man work I've done! Next stop, A$^+$ city!

Wednesday, December 20

Today in class I saw Amy's survey. She just did one, but it was really long with tons of questions, and it was graphed really cool with different colors. Printed across the top was her title: "Women in the New Millennium."

Which, when I thought about it, was just the kind of serious, thoughtful topic Ms. B probably wanted. So I started worrying. What if my surveys are too short? Or silly? Or weird? Or there are just too many of them? What if Ms. B thinks they're stupid? WHAT IF SHE GIVES ME ANOTHER OLD ME C?

So when I got home, I threw away all my surveys. And I spent two whole hours writing down lots of questions about "Men in the Twenty-first Century." Now all I have to do is get some quick answers (I'll go ask Dad) and— BINGO—an A$^+$!

Amy gets to take Ralphster home for the holidays. She's really excited. I've never seen a hamster smile, but I'll betcha Ralphster is happy, too. Knowing Amy, he'll be treated like a king!

Thursday, December 21

Today is the shortest day of the year. So I'll keep this short.

Later,
Thursday, December 21

Well, not as short as I thought. A quick report: As a class we sold 293 chocolate bars and earned $439.50 toward our Incredible-Fantastic-End-of-the-Year Camp-out. Cool.

Eight kids sold more than I did. Good thing I found my real calling, ace-brilliant-type-Question-Man, in the meantime.

Even later,
Thursday, December 21

Okay, okay, so I'm a blabbermouth on paper. But for the record, I just had to write down that Mom and Dad finally asked me what I want for Christmas. They were expecting the usual mile-long list, like greedy Old Me used to give them. But this year, I just said, "Not much. Surprise me."

After she got her jaw up off the floor, Mom said, "You're a good kid, Cody."

Dad nodded. "That he is!"

Wouldn't you write that down, too?

Friday, December 22

Amy was sick today, the last day of school before vacation. I volunteered to take Ralphster to her, since she won the lottery. Ms. B said, "That's very sweet of you, Cody."

Then Ms. B told us to be sure to put our surveys in the homework box. I looked in my notebook and mine was gone. I was sure I'd put it in there, but somehow, somewhere, I'd lost it!

I didn't want to tell Ms. B. This was just

the kind of thing I used to do in fourth grade, and third, and . . . I didn't want her to think I'm still like the Old Me. But then I turned right around and did a dumb Old Me thing—nothing. I didn't hand in anything at all. So now I'll get a big fat zero. Journal title idea: *How Did Cody Get So Stupid?*

Oh well, at least there's no school for two whole weeks. And I've got Ralphster. He's eating a carrot I gave him. Hi, Ralphster! Be sure to tell Amy I fed you well!

Uh-oh, I'm talking to a rodent.

Saturday, December 23

Woke up early this morning to find Emma in my room staring at Ralphster's cage. Her lip was twitching and she had that look in her eye. She was thinking, FOOD!

I threw a sock at her and yelled, "Scat, cat!" She took off. I couldn't get back to sleep, so I got up and made chunky chocolate chip cookies for Amy. I figured it was a good time to return the favor for the ones she brought to me after the election speech disaster. And take Ralphster to her, too—a sort of get well and Hanukkah present all in one!

You'd have thought I brought her the moon. "Thank you, Cody!" she said. She jumped off their family-room couch, where she'd been wrapped in a blanket, watching cartoons. She looked pale and tired, but she was grinning. "You're so sweet!" (That's two times in two days someone has said that to me, so it must be true.)

Then—get this—she gave me a big hug. That's right, a full-blown-arms-all-the-way-around-me hug.

I guess I looked pretty shocked, because I was. Amy stepped back, embarrassed. "Sorry," she said. "I shouldn't have done that. You might get the flu, too."

But you know what? I don't care if I get the flu. I've been hugged lots of times, but I've never gotten a hug that felt like the one Amy gave me. It was nice. *Really* nice. I liked it. *Really* liked it. Just like I *really* like her.

Wait a minute! Did I write that?

Yep, I did.

Which means it must be true.

Whoa! I'd thought there'd be warning signs or something. Instead, one minute I'm going along acting like a regular guy, and then—ZAP!—all of a sudden I really like a girl.

My head is spinning. I'd better go lie down.

Monday, December 25
Christmas Day

I asked Mom and Dad to surprise me with a gift, and they did. They gave me a cool denim jacket. Which I didn't even know I wanted until I unwrapped it.

I wonder what else I don't know I want.

Not underwear, that's for sure, especially Christmas ones with Santas and reindeer all over them. MC acted hurt when I stuffed the ones she gave me under the couch. What did she expect?

Ate too much Christmas ham, but still had room for dessert. Later MC and I watched a science fiction movie about invaders from outer space. MC fell asleep on my shoulder and drooled on my new jacket. Dad said, "Don't worry, it's slobber-resistant."

Thought about calling Amy. But then I found myself thinking, What if she's busy? Or doesn't want to hear my voice? So I hung up.

I had no idea liking a girl was going to be this complicated!

Tuesday, December 26

Finally, I finished my kitty litter box jail term! Today MC had the dirty deed of cleaning up after Emma. I sat and watched her with a big grin on my face.

She only has to do it for one week, though, then it's my turn again. Which doesn't seem fair, seeing as how I just got done doing it *forever*. Still, it sure was fun watching her scoop out those smelly clumps.

Wednesday, December 27

Amy called! She said she's feeling a lot better, but her mom is still making her take it easy. Ralphster is doing fine. Turns out he likes accordion music. When Amy puts on a CD of it, he gets on his exercise wheel and "goes like crazy, like he's dancing the polka!"

I didn't say it (from *Cody's Guide to Girls*: "Don't insult her taste in music") but if Ralphster is like me, he was probably trying to get away from the accordion music, not dance to it.

Thursday, December 28

On the way home from the grocery store, we drove past the park. Tyler and Zach and that bunch of sixth graders—Whit, Nate, Deshawn, and Theo—were shooting hoops. I would have played, too, if they'd have asked me. But it was starting to rain anyway—*again*—so I guess it didn't matter.

Rain, rain, go away, come again some other—No, scratch that. More like: Rain, rain, don't give me no slack. Hit the road and don't come back!

Hey, not bad. Could it be? Ace-brilliant-type-author guy is back?

Friday, December 29

Stumbling into the bathroom this morning, I tripped and almost ended up in the toilet. MC, who happened to be walking by, stopped and looked at me sprawled on the floor. She said, "When a person is in love, they forget how to walk and fall down and can't get up for an hour." Then she busted out laughing. "Cody's in love! Cody's in love! Cody's in love with Amy!"

I shook my fist at her and yelled, "Beat it, bozo brain!"

But I did have trouble getting up.

Saturday, December 30

Went out for dinner tonight. Mexican. Yummy. Except when MC said, "Cody and Amy are going to do the holy matchimony thing."

Dad almost choked. Mom blinked a bunch, then finally said, "Well, no need to rush into anything."

Good point. I think love is fine, but you shouldn't talk about it while someone is eating a taco.

Sunday, December 31
New Year's Eve

All day MC has been running around, saying "Happy New You!" instead of "Happy New Year!" Maybe she's on to something, though. People make New Year's resolutions because they want to change something about who they are. They really are becoming a New You.

Just like I've been working on the New Me. Guess I just started my New Year's resolution a little early, that's all. I'm ahead of my time.

Mom and Dad said I could stay up until midnight and watch the big ball drop at Times Square in New York City on TV. Only thing is that New York City is three hours ahead of us, so when we see it at midnight here, it's already a rerun. Who wants to start the New Year by watching a rerun?

Besides, Mom and Dad will kiss, and I don't want to see any more of that than I have to. Everybody will be kissing at Times Square, too. Kissing, kissing, kissing. Kissing, kissing, kissing.

Almost called Amy to kiss—uh, *wish* her Happy New Year. But I didn't.

Monday, January 1
New Year's Day

Watched the Rose Bowl on TV with Mom and Dad and MC. Ate lots of chips and made lots of noise. It was fun, except that MC kept interrupting and saying stuff like, "I'm the fastest blinker in the family. I can floss my teeth and blink at the same time! Wanna see?" She got all huffy when I finally told her to shut up.

"Patience is a virtue," she snipped at me. Mom and Dad looked at her like they were thinking, Wow, what a smart kid we've got, using big words like that! But then MC said, "What is a virtue, anyway?"

This is going to sound weird, but I can't wait for school to start again.

Tuesday, January 2

Nobody said it out loud, but I could tell I wasn't the only one in my class glad to be back. Everybody was talking a mile a minute. Amy had lots of Ralphster stories.

Ms. B didn't waste any time chatting, though. If she had a theme song for today, it was "Glad-to-see-you-now-get-to-work!" Math, reading, social studies, science—we hit them *all* before lunch.

Friday, January 5

Zach has started calling girls "female life-forms." Amy just laughs, but Libby boils. She called Zach a "meathead life-form."

I'm getting *really* tired of doing Emma's kitty litter box. Sticking that super-dooper-pooper-scooper in there is like going back to jail. There has GOT to be a way out of this.

Think outside the box. Think outside the box. Think outside the box.

Saturday, January 6

Still thinking outside the box. *Still* thinking outside the—

Hey, wait a minute! That's it: outside the box! As in outside the box we call our house! Emma can become an outdoor cat and do her business in the bushes or Mom's flower beds, like all the other cats in our neighborhood!

Duh. Why didn't I think of this before?

Later, Saturday, January 6

I'll tell you why I didn't think of it before. Because according to Mom, "Emma would kill birds that come to the feeder. Cats kill millions of birds a year."

I said, "Emma wouldn't do that. She's nice."

Mom said, "All cats do that. They're not mean; they're predators."

I said, "Well, can't we put a bell on her so the birds can hear her?"

Mom said, "Emma is smart. She learned to turn on the water in the bathroom, remember? She'd learn to stalk without jingling the bell."

I said, "Then we give her more cat food so she won't be hungry."

Mom said, "The urge to hunt and the urge to eat are controlled by different parts of a cat's brain."

I said, "How do you know all of this stuff?"

Mom said, "Because I'm a librarian, and we know everything." Then she went on to tell me the other reasons to keep Emma inside: "She could be run over by a car. Dogs might attack her, or other cats. She could get fleas, ticks, mites, or worms, not to mention rabies, distemper, leukemia, and lots of other fatal diseases."

I said, "That's terrible."

Mom said, "But here's the worst part."

I said, "What could be worse?"

Mom said, "Emma might bring back a bunch of her friends and they'd *all* use her litter box!"

I said, "You're right. That's worse."

Mom said, "I thought you'd see it my way. Now go clean up after our indoor cat. It's your turn."

Moral of the story: Don't try to argue with your mom, *especially* if she's a librarian.

Sunday, January 7

MC said that she and Jordy have decided that Amy and I have to get married so they can be brother and sister. I told her that's not the way it works. And even if it did, it doesn't matter because Amy and I are too young to get married, and we're not going to get married anyway.

MC poked at me with a carrot she was nibbling and said, "Ha! That's what you think!"

I poked right back at her with a piece of celery and said, "Ha! You don't have a clue what I think!"

I think.

Wednesday, January 10

Snow flurries during recess. Everybody went nuts, running around with their mouths open, trying to catch flakes. We were all sure the storm was going to dump two feet and school would be called off, but it stopped.

Dad said that if you wear your pajamas inside out, it will snow, and stick. MC said, "Really?" Dad said, "Yes, and remember, kids, there are three kinds of people in this world: those who can count, and those who can't."

Friday, January 12

I've been thinking about how cool it would be to be invisible. I could spy on anybody I wanted to!

Like Amy.

Don't tell her I said that.

Saturday, January 13

Jordy came over again this afternoon. I asked him why he didn't just move in. He said, "You have to marry Amy first."

MC put her hands on her hips and said, "Yeah!"

I started to bop both of them with a couch cushion, which would have been very Old Me. But then I thought a New Me thought: ignore them. They want me to get mad and chase them (they think that's fun), but if I don't, they'll get bored and go away.

So I ignored MC and Jordy while they chanted, "Cody loves Amy! Cody loves Amy!" And I ignored them while they danced around me humming the wedding march song. And I ignored them while they did a hip-hop rap: "Cody and Amy sitting in a tree, k-i-s-s-i-n-g. First comes love, then comes marriage, then comes Emma in a baby carriage!"

And *then* I bopped them both with a couch cushion.

Monday, January 15

Typed in "cats" and "litter box" on the Internet and surfed around a bit. The next thing I knew there was a picture of a cat using a regular human toilet! It said: "Kitty Whiz Potty Training Kit. No more litter boxes! Includes plastic training form that fits over present toilet seat, bag of attractive herbs, instruction booklet, and diploma."

Wow! And it's only $8.99 plus shipping!

Later, Monday, January 15

I waited until Mom went to her book club meeting to show Dad the Kitty Whiz website. (I figured he'd be an easier sell.) He had to work really hard not to laugh—his ears got red and he puckered his lips.

I asked MC if she'd split the cost of the Kitty Whiz with me. She said, "Sure, then I could take Emma to school and she could go potty for show-and-tell!" But she'd already blown all of her money on an Elvis CD.

I said I'd buy the Kitty Whiz myself then. Dad acted like I was being silly, but finally said, "Okay, if that's how you want to spend your savings." He ordered the kit off the Net with his credit card and I paid him right back. The Kitty Whiz Potty Training Kit will be here in a week to ten days. We'll be rid of that litter box in no time!

Thursday, January 18

Birthday party at school—Zach's. His mom came at the end of the day and gave each of us a cupcake and a choice of pop. I chose Coke, but then my cup got mixed up with Amy's Dr Pepper and I couldn't tell which was which.

Amy said, "Simple!" She thumped each cup on the tabletop. "That's yours. Coke makes more bubbles. See?"

And she was right! Cool trick from a cool girl.

Friday, January 19

For art we took turns tracing the shadows of each other's heads onto a big piece of paper. Then we filled our own profile with pictures cut out from magazines. (That's called a collage, in case you didn't know.) Ms. B said, "Choose pictures that reveal the inner you— what you think and feel and believe."

I didn't even realize I'd glued a photo of a guy and a girl walking hand in hand on the beach until Emerson saw it and said, "Whoa! You've got it bad for Amy, huh?"

I slapped a picture of a basketball player on top of the boy and girl, and said, "No!"

Emerson rolled his eyes, then winked at me like we were in on some little secret together.

We're not!

Sunday, January 21

In church the preacher ended her sermon by asking us to think about how we show someone we love them. MC leaned over and said, "That's easy: you take them out to eat, but then just stare into their eyes until your food gets cold." She wagged her finger at me. "And don't forget her name. And don't have smelly feet."

Wednesday, January 24

MC came running into my room this morning, shouting, "Snow! Snow!"

When I looked out the window, there were big flakes coming down in a blur, sticking to everything. We ran and turned on the radio, and—school had been called off!

It took me a while, but I found the sled in the back of the garage. Dad showed me how to rub candle wax on the runners to make it go faster. I loaded MC on (Mom and Dad said I had to take her with me) and headed for Woodson Park.

Tyler and Zach were there, and Emerson, and Amy and Jordy. They were already having sled races down the big hill. Most of the kids were sitting up on their sleds. I figured that if I lay down, that would cut wind resistance, which would make me go faster. And if MC lay on my back, that would add extra weight, which would make me go even faster!

Tyler said, "Sledders to your mark! Get set! Go!"

We all pushed like crazy. Zoom! We were flying down the hill, the cold air in our faces, whooping at the top of our lungs. MC and I got out to an early lead, and I thought for sure we were going to win. Right at the bottom, though, heavyweight Emerson came flying past us and over the finish line first.

MC threw a snowball at him. Emerson laughed and threw one back. It missed MC and hit Tyler. Tyler scooped up some snow and flung it at Emerson, but it missed and hit Amy. Amy shot one back that ended up hitting me. She grinned and I knew she'd done it on purpose. I threw one at her. She ducked it, then nailed me in the shoulder. Anyway, within seconds all the kids in the park were laughing and throwing snowballs at each other. (Except for Jordy, who kept throwing them at himself and yelling, "Oh, got me!" and falling down.) We had a full-scale war on our hands!

I'm not sure how it ended up with everybody against Tyler and Zach and Amy and me. What I do know, though, is that I've never been so glad to have such bad odds. True, our side had to retreat up the hill under a hail of snowball bullets. And I got hit right in the back of the neck and snow went down my jacket. But once we got behind the boulders, we were able to hold off the charge.

Then I found the bungee cords.

Yep, two of them under the snow where somebody had dropped them, I guess. In a flash of true brilliance, I whipped off my scarf and knotted each end to a bungee cord and— eureka!—we had a BIG slingshot.

Tyler held one end of one bungee cord, Zach the other. Amy and I fitted the biggest snowball we could into my scarf and pulled back. The enemy charged. Amy said, "Wait until you see the whites of their eyes!" Zach grinned. "Yeah, then nail 'em! Especially Emerson!" Just as they topped the hill, Amy said, "Fire!" We let go and the huge snowball went flying and hit

Emerson right in the chest. Hit him so hard it knocked him back into MC. Who got knocked back into Jordy. Who threw another snowball at himself and said, "Oh, got me!" MC jumped up and said, "Hey, you guys, that was no fair!"

Amy laughed. "All's fair in love and war!"

I said, *"Love?"*

By that time Zach and Tyler had a new snow cannonball ready. "Get 'em, you two!" Tyler ordered.

Did we ever. Amy gave me a high five and said, "Cool slingshot, Cody!"

After a lunch of hot soup, I got on some dry clothes and met Amy back at the park. Even though the snow was melting, we sledded and sledded until almost dark, just the two of us. I got home with icicle toes and freezing fingers, and Mom had to run a hot bath to get me warmed back up. But you know what? I didn't care. My toes and fingers might have been cold, but my heart wasn't. I'm in *love* with Amy, and I think she loves me!

Saturday, January 27

Kitty Whiz came today! Dad couldn't stop laughing when he saw the plastic training ring that fits on our toilet seat. He thought the dried herbs I sprinkled in there to attract Emma were pretty funny, too. The diploma I'm supposed to give Emma when she graduates from Kitty Whiz College was what really cracked him up, though. He was laughing so hard he had to leave the bathroom.

Which was fine with me. I had serious work to do. But Emma didn't seem to be interested, not even when I picked her up and stuck her onto the toilet seat. She ran off and hid. I'll try again tomorrow.

Sunday, January 28

Emma still not with the Kitty Whiz program. Maybe I'll give her a day of rest and start again on Tuesday. That'll give me time to read the instruction booklet, too.

I know, you're always supposed to read the instructions first. But hey, I figured, what's so hard about using the toilet?

I wonder what Amy's doing tonight. Maybe I should call and we could just talk.

About what?

Hmm . . . there's a lot to learn about being in love.

Tuesday, January 30

Stayed in from recess and helped Amy clean out Ralphster's TV cage. We took turns holding him while the other one worked. I got to put in the new cedar chips. The old ones smelled yucky, but the new ones smelled good.

When Amy leaned close to put Ralphster back in his cage, I noticed that she smells good, too. Not perfume kind of good, just Amy good.

Wednesday, January 31

Ms. B announced that there will be a talent show in March. It's open to all grades, kindergarten through fifth. Lots of kids are going to try out. Not this kid, though. I can't sing, and the only instrument I play is my CD player. I'm good at running, and basketball, but neither of them are talent show stuff.

Amy and Libby said they're going to try out, maybe sing a song. Amy has a great voice. She's good at everything. MC is going to try out, too. She's going to sing an Elvis tune—"Hound Dog." Can't wait.

Thursday, February 1

Emma hissed and actually tried to bite me this afternoon when I lifted her onto the Kitty Whiz plastic toilet seat. And me trying to make life easier for her. After all, she wouldn't have to scratch around in that dusty old kitty litter anymore.

Friday, February 2

Sat near Amy today at lunch. She laughed when I stuck an orange peel in my mouth so it looked like I had orange teeth. She's got a good sense of humor.

Sunday, February 4

Locked Emma in the bathroom with the Kitty Whiz so she couldn't help but get the Kitty Whiz idea. She pooped on the floor.

Dad says I'm confusing her. Mom says this is not what we need right now. MC says she's glad she didn't waste her money on Kitty Whiz.

Here's what I say: ARRRRGGGGHHHH!

Tuesday, February 6

Dreamed about Amy last night. Saw her first thing at school. Thought about my dream and got embarrassed. She said, "What's wrong?" I said, "Nothing."

Wednesday, February 7

Libby says that Amy says that Jordy says that MC says that I drew a picture of Amy in my journal.

I said, "I don't even have a journal."

Which would make this the *I Don't Have a Journal* journal, which is twisting the truth around in a very Old Me way, I know. But MC made me do it. It's her fault.

Thursday, February 8

Ran relay races in PE. Amy and I were on the same team. I ran first and beat Tyler. Then Libby ran and we fell behind. Emerson ran third (more like waddled, really), and we got *way* behind. Amy ran last. Wow! I didn't know she could run that fast. She passed up Zach, which really bugged him, and we won!

Talent show tryouts were today. Amy and Libby got in, of course. They'll sing a song called "Pizza Love" that is really funny. They're worried, though, because they've only got a month to practice. When they sang it for me, I told them, "It sounds great right now!" and clapped really loud. Amy smiled.

Walked into Mattingly's Department Store this afternoon and they had Valentine's underwear on display—white with red hearts all over them.

No, I am *not* going to get a pair, even if I am in love. No way, no how! End of discussion.

Well, almost end of discussion. I was staring at the heart-covered boxers when a sales clerk in squeaky shoes walked up and asked if I needed any help. Without thinking, I said, "Sometimes I get the feeling that the underwear of the universe are out to get me. Would you mind putting these back in their spaceship?"

Her mouth dropped open. "Uh . . ." was all she could get out before I caught myself and said, "Just kidding."

Friday, February 9

Ralphster got out of his TV cage today during lunch period. (He must have heard we were having burritos and wanted some, too.) Amy discovered he was gone when we came back in from recess. She panicked and almost started to cry.

Guess who found Ralphster under the sink counter? And got a note from Amy with THANK YOU written in BIG letters?

Cody Lee LOVERBOY Carson, that's ME!

Sunday, February 11

I was downtown this afternoon with Mom and MC and saw Amy across the street coming out of the movie theater. I started to yell hello, but then I saw that she was with a boy. They were walking side by side and laughing together.

When I got home, I paced back and forth in my room until I couldn't stand it anymore and dialed Amy's number. Her mom answered and said, "She's still downtown with her cousin."

I said, "Her cousin?"

"Yes, her cousin Taylor from Bend. He's visiting for the weekend."

Oops!

Monday, February 12

Ms. B told us that if we are going to have a Valentine's party, we have to agree to give cards to everyone.

Zach made a face at Libby and said, "*Everyone?*"

Libby made a face back at him and said, "Boys, too?"

Ms. B rolled her eyes and said, "Sometimes I wonder why I got into teaching."

Good question. But right now I don't have time for that. I need to think about Valentine's—which is the day after tomorrow—and what I, Cody Lee Loverboy Carson, am going to give Amy.

Who sat beside me at lunch today and gave me half of her brownie. If that's not a sign of true love, I don't know what is.

Tuesday, February 13

Talk about luck! I went into Richey's Market to get some gum and saw that they had boxes of assorted chocolates on sale. Perfect for Amy for Valentine's! She loves chocolate as much as I do. So I bought one.

But as I was walking home, I started wondering if those chocolates had been on sale because they weren't any good, were maybe stale, or even moldy. Figuring there was only one way to find out, I sat down on the curb and opened them.

First I tried a buttercream caramel. It tasted fine. So I tried a cashew cluster. And an almond nougat. Not bad. And then a piece of the chocolate nut fudge. And Vermont fudge. And toffee chip. Wow! And then a chocolate cordial. And a truffle. Turned out they *all* were great. What a relief!

But now all I had was an empty box and no chocolates. So I went back and spent all the rest of my money on another one. (This is the kind of sacrifice you have to make for true love.)

At home I made a card for Amy and decorated it with a big red heart. Then I wrote a poem in it. (Private stuff, but trust me, it's great writing!) Then I signed it "<u>Love</u>, Cody!" (underlined just like that).

I was admiring my handiwork and imagining how after Amy saw it she'd throw her arms around me, when MC came running into my room (without knocking, of course), pointed a finger at me, and said, "Ha! It's your turn to do the kitty litter box again and it's full of poop!"

I looked around for something to throw at her, and grabbed the empty chocolate box, when all of a sudden I got a brilliant, better idea.

Guess what I'm giving MC for Valentine's Day? Hint: the card doesn't say, "Love" on it, and that empty box isn't empty anymore!

Wednesday, February 14

After breakfast I was sneaking into MC's room to plant my Valentine's "gift" when I heard her coming up the stairs singing that Elvis song she's always practicing for the talent show. So I had to hurry and toss the box and card onto her dresser and hightail it out of there. But I was grinning. This was going to be one of the best gotchas of all time!

All morning at school I looked for an

opportunity to slip the other box into Amy's desk. I wanted all that chocolate and my confession of love to be a surprise.

It wasn't until after lunch that I got my chance, though. While everyone was still in the cafeteria, I acted like I was headed to the bathroom and instead circled back around to our classroom. I peeked in to make sure Ms. B was gone, then tiptoed over to Amy's desk. Mission of love accomplished!

She found my gift when she reached into her desk for her silent reading book. "What?" she said. "Who?" She looked around and I quickly ducked my head and acted like I was already reading. I heard her open the box, and waited for her arms to fly around me—

"You think this is funny?"

I looked up to see Amy rise out of her chair, face red with anger. She stomped over and slammed the box down on my desk.

"You are sick, Cody! Sick! Sick! Sick!"

There was the card I had written MC: "The perfect Valentine's snack for a perfect jerk!" And there, where once had been assorted chocolates, was my gift of assorted cat poop.

Thursday, February 15

Hear Ye, Hear Ye! Listen Up, Everybody!

I, Cody Lee Carson, have an announcement to make: Women—as in female-type persons—are not worth the trouble. I spent the whole day today trying to explain the chocolate box mix-up to Amy, that it was really meant for MC, not for her, that it was just a mistake. But she wouldn't even listen. Zach's laughing at her and telling everybody she got cat poop for Valentine's didn't help. The news spread fast. By lunch today lots of kids were pointing at her in the hall and giggling. Although she acted like she didn't care, she was really embarrassed—I could tell.

Still, you'd think she'd at least give me a chance to apologize.

Saturday, February 17

Okay, no more Mr. Nice Guy. If MC and Jordy are going to keep blabbing about Amy and me, even though Amy still hasn't spoken to me since Valentine's Day, then I'm going to sink to their level, which is lower than a snake's belly while crawling in a ditch, and blab about *them*.

Later, Saturday, February 17

Walked right through the middle of MC and Jordy's card game, singing "Molly loves Jordy! Molly loves Jordy! Molly loves Jordy!"

They didn't even look up.

So I went outside on the front porch and started singing at the top of my lungs: "Molly loves Jordy! Molly loves Jordy! And Jordy loves her, too!"

They didn't seem to care.

I got a big piece of cardboard out of the basement and wrote in gi-huge-o letters: MOLLY LOVES JORDY. Then I carried the sign to the corner and waved it at everybody who passed by, shouting "Extra! Extra! Read all about it! Molly loves Jordy and he loves her!"

Next thing I knew Molly and Jordy were running toward me. Now I'd gotten their attention! They'd beg me to stop embarrassing them. But would I? NO! "Molly loves Jordy, and he loves her! Molly loves Jor—"

MC jerked the sign out of my hands and waved it at a car. "I love Jordy and he loves me!" she sang at the top of her lungs. Jordy chimed in. "And we're going to get married!" They both began to chant, "We're going to get married! We're going to get married!"

Later, as they were trying on dress-up clothes, they thanked me for helping with the wedding announcement. Sometimes it seems like I just can't win for losing.

Monday, February 19

My turn to clean out the litter box again. Twice as much clumped yuck as usual. I think Emma is doing this just to get back at me for the Kitty Whiz thing.

Tuesday, February 20

Went into the boys' bathroom and there was somebody crying in one of the stalls. I knocked on the door and it swung open. Guess who was sitting there?

Jordy. Turns out the reason he was crying was because, and don't ask me why, he'd tied his shoestrings around the toilet paper holder and couldn't get the knot undone!

After I stopped laughing, I said I'd rescue him if he'd promise to stop saying things about Amy and me. He nodded.

I said, "Promise?"

He said, "Cross my heart and hope to die."

So I untied him.

As he walked out the door, he said, "Amy doesn't like you anymore, anyway."

I said, "So what. I don't like her either."

Which is the truth.

Friday, February 23

Didn't get my math done, so I had to go to the library during recess to finish it. As I passed the music room, I could hear Amy and Libby in there practicing "Pizza Love" for the talent show. I stopped and listened, just to see if they were any good.

They're not.

Another bumper crop of kitty litter clumps, and I could swear Emma smirked at me. Rotten cat!

Wednesday, February 28

I was beginning to think that it was impossible for Emerson to embarrass himself. Until today, that is. He had his hand up during math so Ms. B would call on him for the right answer, and all of a sudden he blurted out, "What's that smell?"

Everybody looked at him as he sniffed, and sniffed, and sniffed some more. Then his face turned bright red. Turns out what he was smelling was his own armpit. Zach pinched his nose and said, "Peeuw! Get that boy some deodorant!"

Everybody laughed. Me too, mainly because I wasn't in Emerson's shoes.

Thursday, March 1

If I hear Amy and Libby's stupid "Pizza Love" song one more time I think I'm going to . . . Well, I don't know what I'm going to do. This I do know, though: I'll be really glad when the talent show is over.

Friday, March 2

Dress Like a Movie Star Day. Ms. B wore sunglasses with sequins on them, and kept calling everyone "Darling!" Amy and Libby draped feathered scarves around their necks. Emerson showed up in a black turtleneck and a black French beret. I was going to dress up like an alien from a sci-fi movie, but didn't have a costume. Dad suggested slicking my hair back and turning up the collar of my jacket and going as his hero, James Dean. Which was easy, so I did.

Ms. B said, "Very nice, darling!" and asked me to help with the talent show. "You look like you should be in charge of the curtain and lights. We'd call you Technical Director in Charge of the Curtain and Lights, which is a very important title."

I started to say, "Thanks but no thanks. I don't like being onstage, even if it's behind the curtain." But Ms. B must have seen it coming (she's really good at that). She said, "Don't give me an answer now. Think about it over the weekend, okay?"

Saturday, March 3

Thought about it. Don't want to do it.

Sunday, March 4

Thought about it some more. Still don't want to do it. I'll tell Ms. B first thing tomorrow morning. And that is my final answer.

Monday, March 5

Started to tell Ms. B I didn't want to be Technical Director in Charge of the Curtain and Lights, but chickened out. Tomorrow I really will tell her.
   Really.

Tuesday, March 6

Marched up to Ms. B to tell her I don't want to be Technical Director in Charge of the Curtain and Lights for the talent show. But before I could even get halfway from A to B (much less Z), she said, "I think you'll be perfect for the job, Cody!" Then she walked off.

   Mr. Nosy Emerson, who was standing right there, said, "You don't look so good with your mouth hanging open."

Thursday, March 8

If you know of anyone who wants to learn how to create a really good disaster, send them to me. I'm an expert. No, an artist. Here's how it's done:

THE CODY LEE CARSON GUIDE
TO CREATING
A REALLY GOOD DISASTER

STEP 1. Get chosen to do something you know nothing about, like being Technical Director in Charge of the Curtain and Lights at a school talent show.

STEP 2. Since the light switches and curtain rope are just offstage, where you have a great view of everything, get majorly caught up in watching the talent show acts. For example, say there is a guy named Tyler who is the MC (that stands for Master of Ceremonies, not Molly the Creature). And say that he starts the show by cracking some great jokes, like: "What's invisible and smells like carrots? Rabbit burps!" What you do then is laugh, and forget about the instruction sheet your teacher gave you. So you don't pull the curtain for the first-grade piano player who is so nervous he's about to wet his pants.

STEP 3. After a kid named Libby hisses at you to "Get with it, vacuum head!" you open the curtain. Your teacher, Ms. B, tells the first grader he'll do fine and coaxes him out onto the stage. He sits down at the piano and plays something called "Invention in D Minor" by Bach. And, boy, you can see why they call it that! It sounds like he's inventing it as he goes along. So you laugh some more and forget to turn on the red and blue lights for Jamal, who plays the African drums.

STEP 4. Libby hisses at you again, and after fumbling around and turning on green and yellow lights, you finally find the red and blue. Jamal is great on the African drums, and so you clap and clap and clap, and forget to turn off the red and blue lights like it says there on your instruction sheet.

STEP 5. Which upsets Emerson, who is going to recite Shakespeare. He wants just the spotlights on him. Libby is hissing at you again, which is starting to get on your nerves, but you finally find the spotlight switch. Emerson goes on and on, comparing thee and thou to a summer's day. You get so busy thinking that Emerson should just skip being a kid and become an adult right now, and that he'd probably be a lot happier because he makes a weird kid, that you miss your cue again.

STEP 6. Another method for creating a really good disaster is to turn off the sound system so the microphone goes dead. That way the two magicians on stage both try to fix it at the same time and end up getting into a tug-of-war and rip the mike cord out.

STEP 7. Or maybe you'd want to experiment with closing the curtain right in the middle of Claire playing "Ode to Joy" on the cello, then later opening it while the choir is still getting into place. That will get Mrs. Alonzo, the choir director, flustered and her glasses will fall off and she'll step on them right there in front of everybody. Then Mrs. Alonzo will say something you're not supposed to say in front of kids, and then she'll get even *more* flustered.

STEP 8. Although Libby is still hissing at you and lots of people are now throwing dagger looks your way, the key to creating a really good disaster is not to let up. Now is the time to give it everything you've got! So when Amy and Libby come out to sing "Pizza Love," you should use one of my favorite techniques:

Wait until they get halfway through the first verse and then knock over the music stand Claire left right behind you. It will crash to the floor and distract Libby, who will then forget the lyrics and get really embarrassed. Amy will keep smiling and trying to keep the song going, but it won't work. Libby will be lost. Amy will get lost, too, and finally they'll just sort of fade to a stop. People will clap, but Amy and Libby will walk offstage looking like they want to crawl into a hole and hide . . . right after beating you with a big stick.

STEP 9. Which pretty much sets the tone for the rest of the talent show. Even if you start to goof up and do things just the way they are written on your instruction sheet, people are now so sure their act is going to go bad that it will, even without your help!

STEP 10. True, your sister Molly the Creature is immune to your really good disasters. She'll do her Elvis impersonation perfectly, jumping around onstage with her hair slicked back and lip-synching every word to "Hound Dog" right on time. But most of the sequins she glued on will fall off, and she'll be disappointed when a talent scout doesn't offer her a movie contract after the show. So don't worry, things are still going your way. And keep in mind, the best is yet to come!

STEP 11. That's right. Just when you're thinking it couldn't get any better than this, out onto the stage comes Amy again, this time with juggling balls. You are so surprised—you didn't know she had signed up for two acts—that you just stand there with your mouth hanging open. Of course you are supposed to be turning on the spotlights. But who cares? Amy is tossing juggling balls under her leg. And flipping them behind her back. And throwing them really high. And you're thinking, Wow, she's good! And that maybe you made a mistake about her and you two should make up.

Until Libby hisses right in your ear, "Spotlights, numskull!" And you jump and flip the wrong switch and the stage goes black.

Amy shrieks and you hear three juggling balls hit the floor. Libby screams at you to "Do something!" So you do. You begin throwing every switch you can get your fingers on. Finally, you know you've found the main switch, because every light on the stage flares up in a blinding flash. There is a sizzling sound in the lighting panel, and the whole auditorium goes black. Cool! Now you've *really* done it. You've blown a fuse!

STEP 12. People start to panic. Shouts fill the air. All you can see out there is the red glow of the exit light over the auditorium doors, and you remember that there is a light switch nearby. Maybe it's on a different circuit. You've done a great job of creating a really good disaster, but there could be one last thing you can do to make it even better!

"Don't worry!" you shout. (Which is very funny coming from you.) You jump off the stage and stumble to the exit door, grabbing blindly for the light switch, forgetting that there is a fire alarm right beside it.

Yep, a fire alarm. When all else fails, pull that for a really good disaster. Just ask me. I'm an expert.

Friday, March 9

This morning it felt like spring for the first time, so I decided to ride my bike to school. It was great. The sky was clear blue, not a cloud in sight. The air smelled fresh, and the sun beat warm on my back, and—

Okay, okay, the real reason I rode my bike was because I was seriously thinking about skipping school. Maybe even skipping town, after the disaster last night. I rode along completely ignoring the blue skies and smells of spring. All I could think about was getting away and starting a New Life in a New Me place. But where? Australia would work. Nobody would know me.

Anyway, I was so caught up in planning my

great escape, I didn't see Zach and the sixth-grade boys standing with their bikes at the corner of Cedar and Twenty-third Street until I'd about run into them. I braked hard. "Hi, guys," I said, trying to hide my embarrassment. Yep, Australia, I thought. ASAP.

Zach looked over his shoulder at me and nodded, but quickly turned back to the sixth graders. He was right in the middle of telling them something. "You won't believe what my brother did to me last night," he said.

Whit, the biggest of the sixth graders, said, "If you're talking about Travis, I'd guess he gave you another wedgie, right?"

Zach glared. "Yep. Jerked my underwear up so high I could have used it for a T-shirt."

At the word "underwear" I flinched so bad I almost fell off my bike. To me, it's like someone yelling, "Shark!" at the beach. None of the guys noticed, though. Zach was too much into his story. "I got Travis back this time, though," he said with a big grin. "And the best part is that I didn't have to lift a finger to do it. Mom did it for me. Came right up behind him and gave *him* a wedgie! She told him, 'There, now you know how it feels.' I couldn't believe it. It was great!"

Whit and Nate and Deshawn and Theo all

laughed. I did, too. "That's so awesome!" I said, louder than I meant to.

All the boys stopped laughing and looked at me. There was a long moment of silence, then Whit said, "Hey, aren't you Cody, the kid who pulled the fire alarm at the talent show?"

"Uh . . . well . . ." I started backing my bicycle away from the curb.

"My third-grade sister was in the choir," Whit said, walking toward me. "She said you ruined the whole thing."

I kicked my bike pedal around and put my foot on it. My heart was pounding as I looked around for the best escape route. Australia, *now*!

"Cool," Whit said.

I blinked. "Huh?"

He grinned. "*Very* cool!" And all of a sudden Whit and Nate and Deshawn and Theo were gathered around, giving me high fives, and telling me what a great prank I'd pulled off, and how I had "potential."

Finally, the sixth graders headed off for middle school, but Zach let me ride with him to Garfield. We made a game out of trying to spit in the little holes in the manhole covers. Then in the distance I heard the bell ring and started to pedal faster.

But Zach said, "Cool, we're late."

So I said, "Yeah, cool," and slowed down again. I was tardy and had to go to the office, and got into Old Me double trouble. But you know what? For the first time in my life, I didn't care. It felt . . . well, it felt good!

Saturday, March 10

Mom got kitty litter at the grocery today. Since it's my turn again to clean out the box, I had to completely empty it, scrub it—disgusting!—and put in the new litter. In the meantime, Emma decided it would be fun to pee under the dining room table.

Mom said, "She's still upset from the Kitty Whiz."

"Yeah," Dad said, "probably Kitty Whiz post-traumatic stress syndrome." He laughed like that was supposed to be really funny. I have no idea what he was talking about. But I do know what it all boiled down to: guess who had to clean up the pee in the dining room, too?

Yours truly.

Who has truly had it with that cat!

One more time and I'm putting her up for adoption!

Tuesday, March 13

During science Ms. B said that with a long-enough lever and a pivot to set it on, you can move just about anything, even planet Earth!

Zach said, "Cool! I'm gonna give it a try!"

Libby said, "Where would you move it, Mr. Smart Guy?"

Zach said, "What difference does it make?"

Libby said, "A lot. I live here."

Zach said, "Oh, so maybe I should put a lever under you!"

Later, Ralphster got out again. Emerson found him this time, so he got a thank-you note from Amy. He was grinning from ear to ear, like it was some kind of big deal. He's clueless.

Thursday, March 15

Made farting sounds under my arm today in PE. Emerson said, "Peeuw!" Amy rolled her eyes. But Zach laughed! I had to sit against the gym wall for ten minutes of time-out, but it was worth it.

Friday, March 16

MC and Jordy practiced for St. Patrick's Day, which is tomorrow, by sticking green ribbons up their noses and swinging them back and forth as they marched around the living room.

Mom did *not* think this was funny.

Jordy went home early.

Saturday, March 17

St. Patrick's Day. Not one nostril ribbon in sight. MC actually cleaned out the litter box, but it's my turn again come Monday. Which I don't want to do!

So I got back on the Internet and typed in "cats" and "litter box" again. I surfed around in some different places, and up popped the answer to my dreams: the Littermaid Self-cleaning Deluxe Litter Box! It said, "Never touch, toss, turn, scoop, or clean your cat's litter box again!" Plug it in and an electric eye senses when your cat has used the box. Ten minutes later a rake moves forward, scooping the clumps into a "sealed, airtight container." When the container is full, you just throw it away!

All of which sounded too good to be true . . . until I saw the price: $144.95. Ouch!

Sunday, March 18

Printed out the info on the Littermaid Self-cleaning Deluxe and showed it to Mom and Dad. Dad said, "Sorry, bud. Way too expensive." Mom said, "Not a chance."

"How about as a birthday present?" I said. (My birthday is pretty soon.)

"No, Cody."

"You wouldn't have to get me anything else, or anything for next Christmas, either."

"No, Cody."

"Plus I'd throw in all the money in my sock drawer, too—twenty-three dollars and fifty-five cents!" (I was desperate.)

"No, Cody."

"Pleeeease!"

"No, Cody."

"Don't you know anything else to say besides 'No, Cody'?"

"No, Cody."

Monday, March 19

Tyler's name got drawn out of Ms. B's hat, so he gets to take Ralphster home for spring break. Amy looked disappointed. What does she think, it's *her* hamster?

Tuesday, March 20

I was worried about not having my homework done for science today until Zach said, "Just act like you've got it done." Then he gave a great demonstration. It's pretty easy, actually. All you have to do is keep your eyes to the front of the class, like you're paying attention. Nod your head every now and then. Raise your hand a few times, too, like you want to give the answer. But don't raise it first, only after you see Ms. B is going to call on someone else. Besides that, look confident and smile.

I tried it. It works!

Friday, March 23

Last day of school before spring break. Tyler hit a foul ball at recess that landed on the flat part of the cafeteria roof. Nobody knew what to do about it, until I noticed that the big tree by the cafeteria had a limb that had grown out over the building.

So I climbed up the tree and got the ball. As I was about to climb back onto the limb, Zach said, "Bet you won't jump off into the Dumpster."

I looked down. It didn't seem that far. And besides, the Dumpster was almost full. The trash would cushion my landing. I said, "How much?"

Zach said, "A buck."

After our beloved principal, Mrs. Mead, helped pull me out of the Dumpster and sent me to the bathroom to get cleaned up—lots of left-over spaghetti in that Dumpster, as it turns out—she called Ms. B into the office. Ms. B couldn't believe it when she heard what I'd done. "What has gotten into you lately?" she demanded.

It was a very Old Me moment, until I went back out in the hall. Kids I didn't even know came up to me and said it was the most superstar Dumpster plunge they'd ever seen. I was famous! Plus a dollar richer!

Saturday, March 24

Spring break. So far, so boring.

Later, Saturday, March 24

Ran into Tyler and Zach at the park. We talked for a while, then they had to go to Tyler's house. Still, it was cool.

Sunday, March 25

Saw Tyler and Zach at RJ's restaurant. They were playing the new video game Doom Tomb. Like Zach said, it was "over the top!"
    Spring break—so far, so good.

Monday, March 26

MC came running into my room—without knocking, of course—and said, "Amy and Libby just rode by on their bikes!"

    I went and looked, but they were already gone. MC giggled, so I had to set her straight and say, "Like I care?"

Which is the truth.

Almost told Zach and Tyler about my birthday (it's this coming Sunday) but chickened out. They've probably got plans anyway. And besides, Mom and Dad haven't even asked what I want for a present, much less if I'd like to have a party.

Tuesday, March 27

Mom and Dad announced at breakfast that we are going to the beach. "A surprise vacation," Dad said. "We were both able to get a few days off work."

I said, "I don't want to go."

Which actually surprised me as much as it surprised Mom and Dad and MC. I love the beach. But when I thought about it, I figured that my mouth was just ahead of my brain, that's all. It already knew that I'd rather stay home and hang out with Tyler and Zach, and maybe even the sixth graders, than go anywhere with my family.

We leave tomorrow.

Friday, March 30

Got sick of MC bugging me at the beach and yelled at her to take a long walk off a short pier.

Mom said, "Watch it, Cody. You're headed for trouble."

We finally got back home and found the kitty litter box full to the brim. MC laughed and said, "It's your turn, na, na-na, na-na!" And I sort of . . . well, I guess you could say I really lost my temper and threw a scoopful of cat turds at her.

So now I'm grounded for the rest of spring break, which includes my birthday.

Sunday, April 1

Okay, here's a riddle for you. Picture this: I'd been grounded in my room all day, on my birthday (which seemed about as mean as parents could get). So when Mom called me to come down for dinner, I wasn't in the best of moods. I walked into the dining room, and there was MC piling a mountain of brown sugar on top of . . . a waffle.

"Waffles?" I said. "For dinner?" I love

waffles. They're up there with chocolate chip cookies and pizza on my favorite foods list.

"It's not a waffle," MC explained, "it's a volcano." She poked her thumb into the summit of Mount Sugar, then poured syrup into the crater. "Look, it's erupting!" she said as the syrup oozed down the side.

Of course I ignored her, because she's my little sister, but, more important, because at that very moment Mom was putting two fresh waffles on a plate for *me*.

"Waffles?" I said again. "For dinner?"

Mom smiled and said, "It's your birthday. We thought you'd enjoy a special treat, especially after being grounded. Would you like whipped cream on them?"

"Whipped cream?" I said as she spooned on a mound. "For dinner?"

"How about some strawberries, too?" Dad said. He plopped a big spoonful into the whipped cream.

"And of course maple syrup!" Mom said as she poured a river of the lovely stuff over everything.

I stared, bug-eyed. They'd turned my regular old waffle (which I really like) into a Belgian waffle (which I really, REALLY like). And for dinner! This ranked *above* chocolate chip cookies and pizza on my favorite foods list!

"Oh, and then there's this," Dad said, and laid a hundred-dollar bill in front of me. Yep, one hundred dollars, as in more money than I'd ever had in my entire life. Wow!

Then he added a hundred dollars more.

"Happy birthday, Cody!" Mom and Dad both said, and gave me a double hug.

So the riddle is this: What's wrong with this picture? Yes, what's *wrong* with it?

Any ideas?

C'mon, think, think, think!

Okay then, I'll tell you. What's wrong with the picture is that the waffle was made of Styrofoam. And the "whipped cream" was actually shaving cream. And those strawberries Dad was so generous with were made of plastic. And that maple syrup was motor oil. And those one-hundred-dollar bills were fake!

"April fool!" my family shouted.

They'd gotten me again. It's the curse of being born on April first.

"Not bad," I admitted, "but no more tricks, okay?"

"No more," everybody said, "we promise."

Right. I could see them crossing their fingers

behind their backs. So it didn't surprise me that after our dinner of real waffles, with real whipped cream and strawberries and syrup, Mom brought out cooked cauliflower (my least favorite food ever), then teased me that I had to eat it before I could have any of my birthday cake.

When they finally brought the cake to the table, I was ready for anything: more shaving cream, plastic sherbert on the side. Well, almost anything, except a birthday cake made to look like a kitty litter box.

That's right, a kitty litter box, complete with crumbled white cookies to look like the litter, and Tootsie Rolls to look like . . . well, you get the idea. The joking and pranks went on and on and on. I finally gave up and got into it. Funny thing, as soon as I did, I felt better, and better, until I felt great. We had a grape fight at the dinner table, catapulting them with spoons. (MC started it.) Outside MC and I glued a quarter to the sidewalk, then hid in the bushes and watched people try to pick it up. (Our own little April Fools' trick.)

But the best part was the present from Mom and Dad and my grandpa Irving in Kentucky—a Littermaid Self-cleaning Deluxe Kitty Litter Box! Just like on the Internet. They'd gone in together to give it to me. "In the inter-est of world peace," Dad said.

So anyway, a day that started out looking uglier than ugly turned into a ten!

Monday, April 2

Amy asked Tyler twenty thousand questions about Ralphster's spring break, then kissed him (Ralphster, not Tyler) on top of the head. Zach said, "Blggh!"

I agree.

Tuesday, April 3

To celebrate being back from spring break, Jordy stuck peas up his nose at lunch and blew them into his mashed potatoes.

MC thought this was very funny, until Jordy sucked in by accident and the pea got stuck way back in his nose. He panicked and started digging in there with his little finger, then hacking and making gagging sounds. I thought someone was going to have to do that first aid thing, the Hemlock method or whatever it's called. But all of a sudden Jordy coughed really loud and got this big smile on his face. He opened his mouth. There was the pea on his tongue.

MC clapped and clapped like this was the work of a comic genius. Nope. Just the work of a bozo.

Sunday, April 8

Flipped back to page one of this journal and read what I'd written in September, all that stuff about me becoming a superstar and all that.

Ha! Who did I think I was kidding? Myself, I guess.

No more, though. That kind of talk is for silly kid dreamers. Good thing I've grown up, and am writing like a REAL New Me.

Title idea: *The REAL New Me Journal of Cody Lee Carson.*

Thursday, April 12

Zach picked me to be on his and Tyler's soccer team during recess. "Cody's fast," Zach said. Which was cool.

Emerson wanted to be on our team, too, but Zach said, "No, you'll just get in the way." Which was right.

Still, it felt weird to see Emerson go slouching away.

Friday, April 13

Dreamed Ms. B stood in front of the class and said, "Did someone lose these?" She was holding up a pair of underwear. *My* underwear, and they were alive, wriggling in her hand, calling out, "Cody! Cody!" Everybody started laughing and I screamed, "No!" and woke myself up.

After an Old Me dream like that, not to mention that it was Friday the thirteenth again, I decided to play it safe and stay home. I told Mom I was feeling sick. She bought it without any argument. Which I thought was kind of strange. Until I realized that was because she was feeling sick. Turns out she had the twenty-four-hour flu. Which she was kind enough to share with me. Which just goes to show you: bad luck travels.

Sometimes I wish I could just fast-forward life and skip over the Old Me parts.

Monday, April 16

Ms. B announced today that we'll be having a science fair.

"Science fair?" Zach said, a little too loud, and a little too smart-alecky. Ms. B eyed him for a few seconds, and I thought, Uh-oh, she's going to let him have it.

But she didn't. She took a deep breath like you see teachers do, and then gave us a little handout thingy that explains what we're supposed to do. This is it:

Science Project Procedure

(A) Come up with a scientific question. (For example: How much light is best for spinach plants?)

(B) Devise an experiment to answer the question. (Divide spinach sprouts into groups and place in varying lights, from none to full sun. Observe their growth rates and record data.)

(C) Present your findings. (Display plants, along with an explanation of your experiment and what you concluded.)

Ms. B said, "Of course you'll be more creative than my example! Go wild! Have fun!"

Zach rolled his eyes, then acted like he was dialing a phone. "Hello?" he whispered. "Earth to Ms. B. The fact that we now have even more schoolwork than ever is *not* fun."

Ain't that the truth.

Ms. B says the science fair will be on Friday, June first. Oh, joy. Can't wait.

Friday, April 20

Tonight MC pulled some lint from her belly button and said, "How did *that* get in there?"

Which I figured to be one of the great scientific questions of all time. And would make a great project for the science fair!

To really do it right, though, first I'd have to give some background information: Why we have a belly button, who has one and who doesn't, and I'd use lots of fancy medical terms, like innie and outie. Next I'd go into "Fun Things You Can Do with Your Belly Button," like decorating it, or how to convert it into a secret compartment, or make cool noises with it, or how to belly dance (maybe). And of course I'd have to include "Care of Your Belly Button," which would be full of useful tips on daily maintenance, travel with your belly button, sand and lint removal (that's for MC), climate control, and meeting its social needs.

Then, after really grabbing everybody's interest, I'd hit them with not only the scientific question of belly button lint, but also:

> Why do we have only one belly button?
> What if we had none?
> What do belly buttons do when we're asleep?
> Do belly buttons communicate with one another?
> Do belly buttons ever eat homework?

I'd have an experiment for each scientific question, and even though Ms. B might roll her eyes and shake her head and think I was being silly, Tyler and Zach might think it was cool.

So maybe I'll do that.

Then again, maybe I won't.

Saturday, April 21

Jordy came over today. (Surprise! Surprise!) He and MC went to the park, where they caught seven tadpoles in the creek. Mom let them make an aquarium out of an old plastic bucket. The tadpoles seemed to like it. They swam around a lot.

After lunch Mom took MC and Jordy to her library and they checked out a book on raising tadpoles. The book says that tadpoles eat algae in the wild, but in captivity you can just boil up some spinach and feed them that.

"Spinach?" MC said, and started making gagging sounds. Jordy fell on the floor and acted like he was dying of bug spray. They both put clothespins on their noses and made lots of faces when they were boiling the spinach. It was fun to watch them suffer.

Here's the best part, though: MC and Jordy were so into those tadpoles that they sat around the rest of the afternoon watching them and didn't bother me at all!

Ah, peace and quiet . . . so I could play my CDs REALLY LOUD!

Tuesday, April 24

Ms. B reminded us that we should definitely be getting going with our science fair projects if we haven't already. She started asking who was doing what, and lots of kids were raising their hands and bragging—Emerson, Amy, Libby, Tyler. Ms. B was working her way around the class, and I could see she'd be asking me soon. It was one of those think-fast-or-die moments, and I was getting panicky, when suddenly I had this great idea. My scientific question would be: What is the best way to burp?

Think about it. Some people are definitely better burpers than others. Zach, for example. He can really blast 'em. He claims it's all in the throat, but I think there may be other secrets. I'd come up with an experiment, and have my subjects drink Coke and then burp (my favorite technique), and then try water (not enough fizz?), and then try burping while bending over, or standing on their heads.

I could experiment with location, too. They could burp in the school bathroom (better echo in there?), the cafeteria, the hall, in the back of the bus. Then I could present my findings at the science fair with an all-school burp-off. Yeah! That would be so cool! Tyler and Zach would be bound to laugh at that!

But just as Ms. B was looking my way, the lunch bell rang, so I didn't get to share my great science fair project idea.

Wednesday, April 25

If you look closely, you can see that some of MC and Jordy's tadpoles are growing back legs. Emma was interested in seeing, but MC said, "Don't even *think* about it!" and put her out in the hall. Emma looked up at me and said, "Meow." I'm not much at Catlish, but I'm pretty sure that meant "Me want to eat tadpoles NOW!"

Thursday, April 26

Zach and Tyler got into an argument today, so Zach picked me to be his partner in science lab. Turns out we're really good together. We were the only team in the class that got all the answers right!

So there, Ms. B.

Friday, April 27

Our PE teacher, Mrs. Radicci (we call her Mrs. Radish), said we're going to start square dancing next week. Zach groaned. So did I.

Mrs. Radish said, "I know it may sound odd to some of you, but there are those who actually *want* to dance."

Zach and I rolled our eyes. Who in their right mind would want to do that?

Saturday, April 28

Tried burping while standing on my head and almost threw up. Think maybe I'll find another science fair project.

MC said she and Jordy have adopted the tadpoles, so now they are official members of the family. I said, "Just like we found you in the creek and adopted you!"

She said, "Ha, ha, very funny."

Anyway, she and Jordy have named the seven tadpoles after the seven dwarfs in *Snow White*. So now we have Sleepy, Happy, Dopey, Sneezy, Grumpy, Doc, and Bashful. I took pictures of them with Dad's new camera. We printed them out, so MC and Jordy tacked up the pics on MC's wall.

Monday, April 30

Girls, in case you didn't know, are crazy. Square dancing started today, and turns out they ALL like it. Plus—get this—Emerson said he likes it, too.

Maybe Zach is right. Maybe Emerson really is a complete and total dweeb.

Mrs. Radish assigned partners, and I had to dance with Libby. Libby groaned, so I groaned back even louder. Mrs. Radish told me to be quiet or she was going to send me to the office. She didn't say a word to Libby. Which just goes to show you: men get discriminated against, too!

Anyway, to make things worse, Libby and I had to hold hands. I would rather have grabbed onto a giant slug. But Mrs. Radish looked right at me, so I took Libby's hand. I thought it would be slimy and cold. It was smooth and warm, but weird anyway.

Tuesday, May 1

Ms. B says the chocolate bar sale didn't earn enough money for the Incredible-Fantastic-End-of-the-Year Camp-Out. The campground costs more than she thought it would, and the tour of the fish hatchery, and the natural history museum, too. Plus gas money for the parents who drive. And then there's food. "It takes lots of bucks to feed all of you."

Zach leaned over to me and whispered, "Yeah, especially to feed fat boy Emerson."

Speaking of big eaters, those tadpoles must be gobbling a lot. Their back legs are growing fast! MC and Jordy want to keep track of whose are the longest. I showed them how to chart it all on a graph. MC said, "Neato!" Right now Grumpy is ahead.

Wednesday, May 2

Today in PE Mrs. Radish said that not only do we boys have to hold hands with our square dance partners, but we also have to put our arms over their shoulders when we walk around the square side by side. (That's called a promenade, in case you didn't know.) Libby and I got it okay, but I could tell she didn't like it any more than I did.

Tyler and Zach almost got into a fight over soccer. Zach said Tyler tripped him. Tyler said he didn't. Zach said he did. Tyler said he didn't. Zach said he did. Tyler said, "You argue all the time." Zach said, "No, I don't! You do!" Tyler said, "No, I don't! You do!" Zach balled up his fists. Tyler did, too. And for a minute I thought they were really going to slug it out.

But then Emerson walked up and tripped over his own feet. He flopped face first onto the ground with his big butt sticking up in the air and the top of his underwear showing.

Everybody started laughing. Which would have *completely* fried me. But Emerson just laughed, too, like he enjoyed embarrassing situations. Anyway, with all that going on, Zach and Tyler forgot about their argument.

Thursday, May 3

Zach called me Big Guy today. "Hey, Big Guy!" was what he said. Then he slapped me on the back like we are really good friends.

Which we are, you know.

After school MC came running into my room (without knocking, of course), shouting "Sleepy's got front legs! Grumpy, too!" She grabbed me and dragged me to go see. Sure enough, two of the tadpoles now have front legs. "They weren't there this morning when I got up!" MC said. "It's a miracle!"

While she took a bunch of photos, I looked in her tadpole book and found out that actually the front legs were growing all along, just covered by a thin layer of skin. That's what all tadpoles do. Then they just broke through, and—tah-dah!—four-legged froggies.

Fund-raiser car wash for the Incredible-Fantastic-End-of-the-Year Camp-Out will be a week from Saturday at the Texaco station.

Friday, May 4

Today was Dress Like a Book Character Day. Ms. B's idea. She loves reading. She wore pig ears made out of felt. "I'm Wilbur," she said, "from *Charlotte's Web*!"

I forgot and just came as regular old me.

Still stuck with Libby in square dance. Amy switched partners, though, and ended up with Tyler. Libby whispered, "Bet you're jealous, huh?"

Ha! I didn't care who Amy danced with. I laughed right in Libby's face. Ha! Ha! Mrs. Radish said that if I keep it up, she really is going to send me to the office, no kidding, just try her one more time and see.

Doc the tadpole died. MC and Jordy found

him after school, floating belly-up in the bucket. MC cried. Jordy put his arm around her shoulder and said, "Doc will be in tadpole heaven." They had a funeral with Elvis music and buried Doc in the backyard.

Saturday, May 5

Jordy showed up right before lunch (his timing is always good) with a new Doc swimming around in a jar. He said Amy went down to the park this morning and caught it for him and MC.

Which was a nice thing to do. I guess. If you don't mind frogs. And if you don't have to live with them in the house, like I do.

Still, I would have caught them a new Doc if they'd just asked.

Sunday, May 6

Went over to Zach's house. His big brother Travis has a sign on his bedroom door that says, NO FARTING ZONE! Zach said, "Right. He's the worst farter in the family. I'll bet he farts fifty times a day."

Which was probably an exaggeration. But it got me to thinking: just how many times a day *do* people fart?

Which seemed like a perfectly good scientific question.

Which would make it a perfectly good science fair project, *if* I could figure out a way to count farts. The problem is that most people try to act like they didn't fart. If it's a silent one and not too stinky, they'll just keep on talking, or doing their math, or whatever. How would I count those?

Of course, lots of farts aren't silent. They can come out in one big loud shot. Or two at a time. Or a whole series of little poots. They can blat, or poof, or pop, or fizz, or froot. Sometimes they even sound like a tuba, or a French horn, or what Dad calls a "toot on nature's trumpet." But no matter what style of fart, people try to cover up the noise. They shuffle their feet, or cough, or tap their pencil. It'd be tough not to miss some.

That just leaves counting the smell. Which might seem simple enough, but it would be hard, too. Farts can smell like beans, or a garbage can, or sulfur (which is the worst, in my scientific opinion). And even when one goes really high on the Peeuw scale, let's say an eight or nine, and you know for sure that's a fart you're smelling, the farter will often blame the dog, or just get up and leave the room.

So that would make it pretty impossible to answer my scientific question. Which means maybe this wouldn't make such a perfectly good science fair project after all. Or even just a plain old good one. Too bad. Imagine the look on Ms. B's face (and the grin on Zach's) when I unveiled my display: "The Farting Zone!"

I'd be famous.

Monday, May 7

Today in square dancing we learned to do a grand right and left. Emerson kept getting right and left mixed up. He turned the wrong way and bumped into Libby. I thought she was going to haul off and whack him, but she didn't.

Tuesday, May 8

Got to school a little early this morning. Amy and Ms. B were watching the Hamster Channel.

Ralphster must have been fixing to do a death-defying motorcycle stunt or something extreme, because both Amy and Ms. B looked worried. I wanted to watch, too, but Amy and I don't get along so well anymore.

Wednesday, May 9

Finally, I got to switch partners and get away from Libby. Mrs. Radish put me with Emily, the new girl from Texas who sits in the back of the class and hardly says a word. We learned to twirl and swing. I twirled Emily a little too hard, I guess, and she almost fell down. Mrs. Radish gave me the evil eye again, but Emily smiled and said, "Yeehaw!" Which, when coming from the quietest kid in the class, means I'm a pretty good dancer.

So *there*, Mrs. Radish!

Thursday, May 10

MC said I have stinky feet. I told her she has a messed-up nose. But then I sniffed my soccer shoes and PEEUW! I hate to admit it (and never would to MC), but she's right!

Which got me wondering: So what causes stinky feet, anyway? Dad said, "The stinky feet gremlins." Mom said, "Bacteria. It grows down in your shoes, then gets in between your toes." Which sounded like science talk to me, and all of a sudden I was thinking, Maybe I could do a stinky feet project for the science fair!

I got on the Internet and found a website full of experiments kids can do. It explained how to collect a microscopic sample with a Q-tip. (Just rub it between your toes.) And gave a recipe using stuff from the kitchen to make this gooey stuff they call a "medium" to help your sample grow.

I found everything I needed—chicken bouillon cubes, sugar, yeast—and boiled it so it would be sterile, just like the instructions said. Then all I had to do was let the medium cool, pour it into a canning jar, toss in the Q-tip, close the lid real tight, and—presto!—my project was off and running!

I put the jar in the back of my closet, where it's dark and warm, like the inside of a shoe. If it works, I'll grow lots of disgusting organisms that will stink like my—er, someone's funky soccer cleats. And I can display them at the science fair, and everybody (even Ms. B) will pass out from the smell!

Which would be very dramatic, and very cool.

Title idea for this journal: *The Very Dramatic and Very Cool Life of Cody Lee Carson.*

Car wash Saturday to raise money for the Incredible-Fantastic-End-of-the-Year Camp-Out. Ms. B says, "Be there or be square."

Be square? Must be old-person talk.

Saturday, May 12

Great day for a car wash—sunny and warm. We cleaned nineteen cars. Most people gave us five dollars or so, but some gave us extra when they heard what we were earning it for. And then Amy's dad donated some more cash, just because. So altogether we earned $132.

Which, added to the $439.50 we earned on the chocolate bars, gives us $571.50!

Which Ms. B said was *finally* enough for our Incredible-Fantastic-End-of-the-Year Camp-Out. We celebrated by spraying her with water. Zach really got her. He's a good shot. Only problem was, Ms. B's a better shot!

Found Emma hanging around MC's door again. Shooed her away, but later she snuck right back.

Monday, May 14

Got partnered up with Amy in square dancing today. She acted like there was nothing weird about it, so I did, too. Mrs. Radish tried to teach us a move called "duck for the oyster, dive for the clam." It sounded more like a seafood dinner than a dance to me and was pretty complicated. Amy and I got it right, though, and Mrs. Radish rewarded us by making us demonstrate for the whole class. Amy seemed proud and smiled at me for the first time since Valentine's Day. I smiled back.

Tuesday, May 15

Ms. B says we'll leave for our Incredible-Fantastic-End-of-the-Year Camp-Out on Thursday, June seventh, and not come back until Friday afternoon. Yahoo!

Speaking of Mother Nature, she sure can pull some pretty weird tricks. Tonight MC came busting into my room near tears and said, "Grumpy's tail is shrinking!" Then she dragged me to look. "See? It's shorter today than it was yesterday!"

I looked in the tadpole book and found out it's called tail resorption. Which is just fancy scientific talk for eating your own tail. Not like hey-this-is-good-please-pass-the-ketchup kind of eating. More like I've-had-enough-of-this-spinach-diet-you've-been-feeding-me kind of eating. In the meantime, I'll just live off this tail of mine. Won't need it anymore once I get to be a full-blown frog, anyway!"

MC broke into a big grin. "Wow!" she said.

I watched her take more photos for her froggie album, then I found myself thinking, Wow is right. This would make a *great* science project, better than anything so far! And the greatest thing about it is that it's already done. They've got that graph (that I helped them make) and a ton of photos (that I taught them how to take). All I'd have to do is come up with the scientific question, which would be . . . How can Cody get his project done with the least amount of work?

Wednesday, May 16

I waited until after breakfast to ask MC if I could use her frogs and the photos and the graph. She said, "No." She's just playing hard to get. Give me a little time, and I'll have her *begging* me to use them!

Thursday, May 17

During math Zach walked past Emerson's desk and put a sticky note on his back that said, "Pinch me!" Emerson peeled it off, changed "pinch" to "kiss," then slapped the note back over his shoulder.

Zach said, "Don't hold your breath, widebody." But at lunch I saw Amy give Emerson a Hershey's Kiss, and they both laughed.

Maybe I should get some sticky notes, too.

Friday, May 18

If I never square-dance again for the rest of my life, that would be too soon. Today when Mrs. Radish said, "Swing like thunder!" I did just what she said, and Amy and I bonked heads.

Amy said, "You did that on purpose!" Then she started to cry.

I tried to explain to her and to Mrs. Radish that it was just an accident, and that I really and truly didn't mean to do it, because really and truly I didn't!

But Amy wouldn't even look at me, and Mrs. Radish said, "I've warned you enough," and sent me to the office. Ms. B found out, so now she's mad at me, too. She says that if I don't get my act together, I can't go on the Incredible-Fantastic-End-of-the-Year Camp-Out. I'll have to sit in Mr. Malcombe's room for two days and do nothing but worksheets.

Thanks a lot, Amy! You are nothing more than a pain in the gazoobie! Mrs. Radish and Ms. B, too!

Saturday, May 19

All the tadpoles are now looking more like little frogs. In just four days their tails have almost all gone bye-bye. I told MC they were superstars, for sure. She smiled.

See, I'm winning her over already.

Monday, May 21

Libby came up to me today at recess and said, "Why did you hurt Amy?"

I said, "Amy who?"

Libby rolled her eyes and called me something under her breath.

Like I care. Ha!

Wednesday, May 23

Emerson gets to take Ralphster home for Memorial Day weekend. When he learned his name had been drawn, he told Amy not to worry. "Ralphster will be in the best of care."

Amy didn't look at all convinced.

Thursday, May 24

Heard the awfulest noise coming from MC's room today. Sounded like a sick cow. Went in to find my little sister with her head in the tadpole bucket.

"Are you okay?" I said.

Head still in the frogarium, MC sang, "Yeah-yeah-yeah! I'm s-s-singing, singing Elvis with my fr-fr-frogs."

I thought, Please st-st-stop, but seeing as how I need to use her fr-fr-frogs, instead I said, "Oh, that's nice. They like Elvis tunes too, huh?"

I bent over the frogarium and listened. What I heard wasn't Elvis—duh!—but little froggie sounds. Not *ribbit,* like you see written in books. More like *kreck-ek, kreck-ek.* "Cool!" I said, and I actually meant it, because it was.

MC smiled like moms do when someone compliments their baby. But she still said no when I said I thought her frogs would like to sing for my science project.

Friday, May 25

After I handed in my math today, I asked Ms. B if I'd straightened up enough to go on the Incredible-Fantastic-End-of-the-Year Camp-Out. She looked at me real hard and said, "So far, so good."

I said, "Whew!"

She smiled, but then said, "That's only if you keep behaving, though."

I said, "I will!"

She said, "*And* get all of your assignments done, especially your science fair project."

I said, "I will!" But inside I was thinking, Yikes! Very-cool-ace-brilliant-type-science-guy had better get MC to let me use her frogs, and I'd better do it NOW!

Saturday, May 26

Today was Mom and Dad's anniversary. They've been married sixteen years, so they finally went out for dinner, just the two of them. Since I'm now eleven, I baby-sat MC. We made a Happy Anniversary card and taped it to the front door so Mom and Dad would see it first thing when they came home. Then we watched TV.

MC started getting sleepy about eight-thirty, but didn't want to go to bed since Mom and Dad had said she could stay up until nine. She asked if she could lie down on the couch until then.

I said okay, so she went up to her room and got her blanket and her stuffed dinosaur, Googlie. I was reading her a story when into the family room walks Emma with something in her mouth. MC said, "Emma, what have you got—no!"

It was a frog.

"No!" MC screamed again, and Emma dropped her prey. Which hopped under the couch.

"Grumpy!" MC said, scrambling after it on her hands and knees. "It's Grumpy! Come here, Grumpy. Come here, little Grumpy!"

Grumpy wasn't interested in saying howdy at the moment. He was interested in staying alive. Emma was stalking him on her belly.

"Emma, leave the frog alone!" I yelled, poking at her. Emma ignored me and lunged for Grumpy. Grumpy leaped and went flying past my ear. Emma darted out after him. I whirled and lunged for Grumpy just as Emma pounced. My leg banged into Mom's reading lamp. Which fell over and crashed onto the coffee table. The lightbulb went *pop* and exploded in a big flash of blue light. Emma screeched and took off like she'd been plugged in. MC started to cry. "I left the door to my room open and Emma got in! I'm a bad mother! Grumpy got killed!"

I sat there blinking for a minute, then opened my hand. "No, he didn't," I said. "Look! He's okay!" I had made the greatest one-handed froggie catch of all time, plucking little Grumpy right out of the kitty jaws of death. It was New Me spectacular.

"Oh, Grumpy!" MC said, grinning through her tears. "Grumpy!" She hugged me and gave me a big old sloppy lip kiss on the cheek. I was about to say, "Yuck! See if I do anything nice for you again!" But then I saw that the door of opportunity was open before me, and said,

"Does this mean I can use your frogs for my science project?"

MC cuddled Grumpy and said, "Maybe."

Which is really just MC's way of saying "Definitely."

Sunday, May 27

Shouldn't have watched that sci-fi movie last night. It gave me nightmares. I dreamed about giant underwear invading Earth. They stomped down Polk Street right up to my house, and peeked in my window with searchlight eyes. I hid under the bed, but it was no use. A giant alien hand crashed through the wall and grabbed me. The next thing I knew, I was in a glass display case on Planet Underwear wearing nothing but Tweety Birds, and all the giant underwear was staring at me with their searchlight eyes. It was creepy!

Tuesday, May 29

Emerson showed up at school this morning looking sadder than a burned biscuit. When Ms. B asked what was the matter, he said, "It's Ralphster."

Amy gasped and put her hand to her mouth. "Oh, no!"

Emerson blinked back a tear, gulped, and then told us that when he looked in the cage Saturday morning, Ralphster was lying on his side and wouldn't get up, not even for Cheerios. They took him to the vet, but the vet said Ralphster was just getting old, and there was nothing that could be done. Emerson stayed up most of the night Saturday looking after him, but he died anyway. Ralphster the hamster is dead and buried in Emerson's backyard.

Amy started crying and couldn't stop for a long time. Ms. B looked teary, too, but forced a smile and said we should be thankful Ralphster had such a full and happy life.

MC heard about Ralphster from Jordy. She asked me if a cat got him. I said no, but she didn't look convinced. She stood guard by the frogarium with a broom to sweep Emma into the next galaxy if she attacked again.

Wednesday, May 30

Went down for breakfast this morning to find MC grinning like a dog at a fire hydrant festival. "I feel so much better," she said between heaping spoonfuls of oatmeal, "since I let my froggies go."

I was still partly asleep (I've been known to wake up *after* I finish breakfast), so it took a few seconds for her words to sink in. When they finally did, I woke up fast. "You did *what?*"

MC smiled proudly. "I couldn't stop worrying about them, so early this morning I let them loose in the creek in the park. I said, 'Be free! Be free!' and they all hopped away!"

ARRRGH! Two days until the science fair. No project = no Incredible-Fantastic-End-of-the-Year Camp-Out. What am I going to do?!

Thursday, May 31

Worried all day yesterday about my science project. Went to sleep worrying about it. Woke up this morning worrying about it. Got up before dawn today and paced. Flopped on the floor and stared at the ceiling. Got mad and threw a shoe. It bounced off the dresser and landed by my head. And that—miracle of miracles—is when I remembered stinky feet!

I found the jar still in the back of my closet, right where I'd left it in early May. There was the Q-tip, right where I'd put it in the "medium." With trembling fingers, I unscrewed the lid. "Please let it stink," I prayed. "Please!"

Does it ever! It's easily a 9.9 on the Peeuw scale. I almost fainted. It's the best, most beautiful stink I ever smelled in my whole life!

Later, Thursday, May 31

Worked on my stinky feet project every chance at school. Raced home afterward and went straight to my room. Worked harder. Did everything Ms. B wants. Stated the scientific question: Why do feet stink? Have my stinky feet jar for the experiment. Made a poster for the display with a picture of a foot. Colored it in to look stinky, with lots of purple and scummy greens and browns. It may not be exactly what you had in mind, Ms. B, but it's done, and that's all you said I had to do. Look out, Incredible-Fantastic-End-of-the-Year Camp-Out, here I come!

Friday, June 1

Unveiled my stinky feet project today at the science fair. You should have seen Ms. B's face. Her eyes got real wide, and her eyebrows went up (which is a good sign, in case you didn't know).

Zach said, "Way cool, Cody!"

So now I'm Way Cool Cody Lee Carson! Who called Mom from school, and she said it's okay for Zach to spend the night tonight.

Yes!

Saturday, June 2

Zach just left from the sleepover. We had a great time. Turns out he likes sci-fi movies, just like me. He brought one I'd never heard of: *Attack of the Killer Tomatoes,* which is a goofy spoof of all those low-budget, grade B (or Z) flicks. We laughed so hard, our sides ached.

It inspired us to launch our own alien attack, on MC. It was Zach's idea. We held flashlights under our chins so we'd look scary, and then busted into MC's room drooling and making killer tomato noises. You should have seen MC jump. Mom and Dad got mad, but it was worth it. Zach said MC deserved to get scared after what she did to my frog project.

We sat up for a long time after that, whispering and laughing. Zach told lots of good stories about pranks he's pulled. Like the time he put flour on top of the blades of his cousin's ceiling fan. And the time he filled his third-grade teacher's umbrella with confetti, so when she opened it at the end of the day, little bits of paper rained down all over her. Personally, I don't think I'd have to nerve to do that, but Zach said, "It was no biggie."

Sunday, June 3

MC said she's going to get me back for scaring her. "Just you wait, Cody!"

When I told Zach, he said, "Ha! Her and whose army?" Which is right. What can a kindergartner do to a fifth grader? Flashlights under the chin do *not* scare Way Cool Cody Lee Carson.

Monday, June 4

Today Ms. B drew names out of two hats—one for girls, one for boys—to divide us into tent partners for the Incredible-Fantastic-End-of-the-Year Camp-Out. Zach and I got drawn to be together.

We started whooping it up, until Ms. B said, "We have an odd number of boys." And she put Emerson in with us.

Zach cussed under his breath, but then grinned and raised his hand and said, "My tent isn't big enough for three, Ms. B." He whispered to me, "Especially when one person takes up as much room as Emerson."

Emerson shrugged. "That's okay. I've got my own tent."

He's going to cook with us, though, so we still had to plan our meals with him.

Ms. B budgeted eight dollars per person for groceries for the trip. Between Zach and Emerson and me, we'll have twenty-four dollars to spend. Ms. B said we had to come up with a "balanced menu." She drew a picture of the food pyramid on the board. (You know: grains, fruits, veggies, protein, all that stuff.) Pointing to the smallest part, she said, "You'll notice that fats, oils, and sweets should be used only *sparingly*. You may plan a small dessert for Thursday night—s'mores are my personal campfire favorite—but *only*"—she really hit on that word—*"only* if you have left-over money after buying all the nutritious foods you need."

Emerson said, "Can we bring extra candy or cans of pop from home?"

Ms. B said, "Absolutely not!" She looked around the room at each and every one of us. "Promise?"

We all nodded—"Promise, Ms. B!"—but Zach crossed his fingers under his desk.

Tuesday, June 5

Finished planning our menu first thing this morning. Ms. B gave us our cash, and the entire class marched to Richey's Market to buy groceries. As soon as Zach and Emerson and I hit the doors, we took off like men with a mission.

We shopped for dinner first. Zach got the bologna and hot dogs and canned chili (protein, Ms. B!). I went for the buns (grains). Emerson loaded up on Pringles, ketchup, and mustard (which are all veggies, in case you didn't know). Then we met at the produce section to pick out fruit.

But Zach doesn't like bananas. Emerson doesn't like pears. And I don't like apples that much. We were standing there arguing over what to buy, when Zach had a brainstorm. "Gummy bears! They're made with real fruit juice. It says so right on the package." We went and looked, and Zach was right. It *is* fruit! So we got three.

Emerson said, "How about we get some more nutritious food like that for lunches and snacks!" So we did: candy *corn* (veggie), Cheetos (cheese = protein), jelly *beans* (more protein), pea*nut* M&M's (nuts = even more protein), and more gummy bears (fruit).

Then we did the same for breakfast: powdered and chocolate-covered doughnuts (made from flour = grains), beef jerky (protein), frosted strawberry Pop-Tarts (strawberry = fruit), topped with maple syrup (comes from a tree, so it must be fruit juice).

When we were done, Zach surveyed our haul and said, "Are we good shoppers, or what?" I said, "We're so good we could get paid to shop for people!" Emerson said,

"Yeah!" We gave each other high fives, and grinned at how clever we were.

Until Ms. B came around the corner. She took one look at our shopping cart and rolled her eyes. Then she made us put *all* the candy back. Which was a good thing, actually, because we were way over budget, as it turned out.

Still, what kind of Incredible-Fantastic-End-of-the-Year Camp-Out was this going to be without any *real* food? As we were grumbling our way through the checkout line, though, Zach whispered to me, "Don't worry, I'll bring survival rations."

Wednesday, June 6

I'm finally done packing for the Incredible-Fantastic-End-of-the-Year Camp-Out. Got everything on Ms. B's list of stuff to bring. And all in one suitcase, just like she said. Oops! Except for a flashlight. Better go ask Dad if I can borrow his. Later!

Came back upstairs just now to find MC and Jordy running out of my room, giggling like sick hyenas. "Stay out of there!" I yelled. I checked to see what they'd messed with, but everything looked okay. Little curtain climbers. They should mind their own business!

But anyway, I won't have to put up with MC and Jordy for two whole days. Yahoo! Tomorrow Way Cool Cody Lee Carson is *finally* off on the Incredible-Fantastic-End-of-the-Year Camp-Out. This is going to be so much fun!

Friday, June 8

There are times in life when no matter how carefully you plan for things to go right, just about anything that can go wrong will go wrong. This is called Murphy's Law. I've never met Mr. Murphy, but whoever he is, he must have been thinking about our Incredible-Fantastic-End-of-the-Year Camp-Out when he came up with his law. Read on. You'll see what I mean. . . .

Ms. B's Carefully Planned Schedule for Things to Go Right: 8:30—Roll call, then load cars in the Garfield parking lot.

Life According to Murphy's Law: 8:30—Stuff is scattered all over the classroom: sleeping bags, suitcases, coolers full of food, kids, parent chaperones with mugs of coffee. Everyone is talking at the same time. Except Emerson, who is late. Zach teases Libby about her Super-woman sleeping bag. Amy tells Zach to be quiet. Zach tells Amy to be quiet. Ms. B tells everybody to be quiet. Everybody talks at the same time. Except for Emerson, who is still late.

Ms. B's Carefully Planned Schedule for Things to Go Right: 8:45—Convoy of cars leaves for the Metolius River fish hatchery.

Life According to Murphy's Law: 8:45—Emerson is still missing. Ms. B sends Libby to the office to call him and see what's up. Sends the rest of us to the parking lot to load cars.

Zach and I are assigned to Amy's dad's mini-van, whether we like it or not. We climb into the backseat. Amy stakes out the middle for her and Libby. When Libby shows up from calling Emerson, Zach says, "Rats! I was hoping you'd gotten lost!" Libby and Amy both glare.

9:12—A backpack the size of an elephant appears, with Emerson under it. It takes another fifteen minutes to tie his mountain of gear on top of the van. But at least all kids are now accounted for. Ms. B tells the drivers, "Stay together in a convoy." And we are *finally* on our way.

9:27—Zach pretends to blow snot in Amy's and Libby's hair. Amy and Libby act like he doesn't exist.

9:43—Zach gets out a marker and piece of paper and writes "Help! We've been kidnapped!" I hold it up in the window so other cars can see. We act like we are screaming to be rescued.

9:55—Zach says, "This curvy road is making me sick!" then acts like he is barfing down Amy's and Libby's backs. I add some good sound effects. Amy and Libby act like we don't exist.

10:23—Emerson has to pee, *now*. Convoy of cars pulls over at gas station. Zach and I hassle Amy and Libby some more. Libby calls me a "dork accessory." I smile and say, "Thank you, ma'am!" Amy still acts like we don't exist.

Ms. B's Carefully Planned Schedule for Things to Go Right: 10:30–11:30—Educational tour at the Metolius River fish hatchery.

Life According to Murphy's Law: 11:15— Still a *bunch* of miles from the fish hatchery, Amy's dad, and Ms. B, and several of the other convoy drivers change the back tire on our minivan. Zach and I lead the class in a roadside song: "Great big globs of greasy grimy gopher guts, mutilated monkey meat, little tiny birdy feet, great big globs of greasy grimy gopher guts, guess I'll go eat worms!"

Ms. B's Carefully Planned Schedule for Things to Go Right: 11:30–12:00—Lunch by the Metolius River.

Life According to Murphy's Law: 12:07—All cars actually arrive at the fish hatchery, but the fishy guy who was going to take us on a tour has given up and gone home to eat lunch. At the sound of the word *lunch,* Emerson starts whining that if he doesn't eat his soon, he'll faint. Ms. B lets out a long sigh. No tour. We eat.

Ms. B's Carefully Planned Schedule for Things to Go Right: 12:00–1:00—Travel to Tumalo State Park campground.

Life According to Murphy's Law: 12:23— Finished with his lunch, Zach starts poking around and spots a small garter snake sunning itself on a rock. He catches it and puts it in my empty Pringles can. He offers chips to Amy. Amy says, "Not on your life." Emerson goes for it, though, and we have a good laugh when he screams and Ms. B tells him to quiet down. We all get in the cars and take off, get lost twice, but finally make it to the campground, over an hour late.

Ms. B's Carefully Planned Schedule for Things to Go Right: 1:00–2:00—Set up camp.

Life According to Murphy's Law: 2:05—
Glad to finally be there, kids go nuts and run around the campsite, checking it out. It's cool, except for the nearby toilet, which is one of those stinky Porta-Potti things. Emerson says it looks like an outhouse on skis, what with the wooden runners on the bottom. Zach says those are so it can be moved easily. I say as long as it doesn't move backward, especially with me in it, because it's sitting at the top of a hill. Ms. B says, "Enough enlightening discussion. Get your tents set up."

Which Zach and I do in less than five minutes. Zach claims the grassy, soft side to sleep on. I don't mind. The lumpy side has the best view of Amy and Libby looking confused as they try to set up their tent, and an even better view of Emerson's tent falling down.

Because that's what keeps happening. He gets done with the job and walks around looking really pleased with himself, then trips over one of the ropes, pulling the stake out of the ground, and *flop,* down the whole thing goes.

It's great entertainment. Emerson gets all huffy when we laugh at him, and says he can do it, he's been camping "thousands" of times. The fourth flop gets us laughing so hard, he yells at us. Which is *really* fun.

Until Ms. B says, "Since you're so great at putting up tents, you can help Emerson. And Amy and Libby, too, for that matter." So we have to, and Amy and Libby and Emerson act like it's fair, even though it isn't. Murphy's Law again.

After all that slave labor, I say to Zach, "Let's go exploring." Emerson says, "Yeah!" and tags along, whether we like it or not. We wander down to the creek, where we skip rocks. Zach gets his to skip eleven times!

Zach finds a long limb on the ground that he uses for a pole to vault over the creek, which is cool. So I do it, too. Emerson walks back and forth looking worried. Zach says, "Good, he's not going to come with us!" But then Emerson finds a log to cross on. It looks slippery, but he puts one foot out on it and doesn't slip. So he puts another foot out and inches toward the center, and doesn't slip. He grins and says, "Hey, look at me!" and slips and falls into the creek.

Zach and I take off running and pole-vaulting through the woods, and are laughing our heads off. Until Murphy's Law kicks in again and we realize we're lost. We wander around for about thirty minutes before we finally pole-vault into the campsite again. By which time we've missed all of *Ms. B's Carefully Planned Schedule for Things to Go Right Nature Walk* and half of *Ms. B's Carefully Planned Schedule for Things to Go Right Ecosystems Class*.

Ms. B isn't happy. Zach says that it's Emerson's fault we are late. Ms. B says, "You are one hundred percent responsible for your own reality." While I'm trying to figure out what that means, Zach gets mad and kicks at Emerson's tent stake and the whole thing falls down again. Ms. B makes him go sit by himself under a big pine tree.

The rest of ecosystems class isn't nearly as exciting, but thankfully has to be cut short. Because then we will *finally* be back on *Ms. B's Carefully Planned Schedule for Things to Go Right* (5:00–6:00—Fix dinner and clean up).

"Whew!" says Amy. As if just being back on *Ms. B's Carefully Planned Schedule for Things to Go Right* means things actually will.

Fat chance! *Life According to Murphy's Law*: Emerson's hot dog falls off his stick into the fire. He rolls it out onto the ground, picks it up, blows off some of the dirt, and deposits it into a bun and chomps away. Libby says, "Disgusting!" and for once I agree. Emerson shrugs. I move to the other end of the picnic table.

Where Zach is making fun of Amy and Libby's dinner of fresh salad, pasta with pesto sauce, and sourdough bread. He says, "That's sissy food. *Real* campers cook *real* camping food like this!" He lifts the lid of our cooking pot to reveal a big glob of burned chili. Into which a bug immediately flies.

Libby and Amy think this is very funny. "Mmm!" they say, "that looks *real* yummy!" Zach starts to look a lot like an insulted grizzly bear, and I think, Uh-oh.

But then he brightens up and says to me, "Forget the chili. This way we'll have more room later for the main course." By which he means all the candy and pop he's smuggled along in his suitcase. All during capture-the-flag and campfire songs and a trip to the stinky Porta-Potti, I think about how hungry I am, and how great all of those goodies are going to taste. Forgetting about . . .

Ms. B's Carefully Planned Schedule for Things to Go Right: 9:30. Bedtime. Lights out. No talking.

Life According to Murphy's Law: Come on! What adult really expects kids to be quiet and go to sleep at 9:30 on an Incredible-Fantastic-End-of-the-Year Camp-Out? Zach and I have some serious junk food eating to do. We chomp on Reese's peanut butter cups, Snickers bars, York Peppermint Patties, and pure milk chocolate, all the time talking a mile a minute about how good it is.

Libby comes over and asks us to please be quiet, we are keeping her and Amy awake. Zach just laughs, and as soon as she leaves pulls out the extra bag of marshmallows. "Let's play chubby puppy!" he says. "You put a marshmallow in your mouth and say 'chubby puppy.' Then, without chewing and swallowing the first marshmallow, you put another one in and say 'chubby puppy' again. The winner is the person who can hold the most marshmallows in his mouth and still say 'chubby puppy.' It's a great game."

In the middle of chubby puppy, Libby comes over again and tells us to be quiet, "Now!"

Zach sticks his head out of the tent and acts like he is going to spit marshmallows at her.

Libby jumps back and says, "You are so gross. I ought to tell Ms. B!"

Zach just laughs.

After Libby stomps off, Zach says, "Speaking of gross, last summer my mom ate a little green caterpillar that was in her salad." Which reminds me of the time my mom found half a worm in an apple she was eating, and almost threw up. Which reminds Zach of the time his big brother drank a whole gallon of root beer on a bet, and *did* throw up. Which reminds me of the time I took a big swig of the Coke at a picnic and there was a fly in it, and I threw up, too. Which reminds Zach that he smuggled along a few Cokes, and he'll give me one if I promise not to throw up. I say, "It's a deal!" And I get so busy thinking about how nice that is of him, and that he really is a generous person, and people just don't understand him, that I don't notice him shaking the Coke up before he hands it to me.

When I pop the top, it goes off like a geyser and soaks me. Zach hoots, "Gotcha!" I quickly peel off my pants and shirt and open up my suitcase. I'm not in such a good mood by then, but am thinking, I sure am glad I packed that extra change of clothes. Instead of my favorite Imadude jeans and Nike sweatshirt, though, what I find makes me break out in an instant sweat. My suitcase is completely crammed with nothing but underwear. Yep, underwear. My underwear. Dad's underwear. Mom's underwear. MC's underwear. Nothing but underwear.

"Molly!" I say between clenched teeth, trying to act angry instead of freaked. "So *this* is what she and Jordy were doing in my bed-room before the trip. ARRRRGH!"

Zach thinks this is the funniest thing he's ever seen, though. He laughs so hard he can hardly breathe. "Haw! Haw! What a gotcha! A suitcase full of underwear! Haw! Haw!"

"It's not funny!" I yell at him. "Because of you and your Coke joke, I don't have anything to wear!"

Zach laughs even harder. "Sure you do!" He grabs the suitcase and starts pulling out pairs of underwear and forcing them onto my arms. "See? There's a new shirt!" And onto my head. "And a new hat!" I am pulling them off and telling him to stop, I REALLY don't like it, but he keeps putting them on faster. "Look out!" he hoots. "Mutant underwear are attacking! Haw! Haw!"

"*What* is going on in there?"

Zach and I both jump. It's Ms. B, and she doesn't sound happy. Zach starts scooping up all the junk food goodies, while I dive headfirst into my sleeping bag. I hear the tent door zip-per. "You've got candy!" Ms. B says, and I scrunch down even farther in my bag. "I told you no junk food! Give it to me!" I hear her grabbing our real guy camping goodies. "You two are absolutely pushing the limits! One more thing and you're in big trouble!" she barks. "Now BE QUIET!" And she is gone.

"Whoa," I whisper, sticking my head out of hiding. "She was steamed. Guess we'd better really get to sleep, huh?"

"Libby told on us!" Zach hisses. He shakes his fist toward her and Amy's tent. "Now we've lost all our survival food, and it's her fault. Nobody does that and gets away with it. She's going to pay!"

And all of a sudden I've had enough of Zach and the grizzly bear look in his eye. He just doesn't know when to quit. He's over the edge. "Hey, forget it," I say. "I don't want any more trouble with Ms.—"

"Wimp!" Zach sneers at me. "If you're not man enough to defend your honor, then *I'll* do it!" He sticks his head out of the tent. "There goes Libby into the Porta-Potti. Perfect! I'll get her good!" And before I can get a word in edgewise, he scrambles out of the tent, scoops up a piece of firewood and the pole we used to vault over the creek, and runs to the Porta-Potti.

"Hey!" I whisper after him. "What are you going to—"

Zach slams the piece of firewood onto the ground, then quickly wedges the tip of the pole over the top of it and under the front edge of the Porta-Potti. The other end of the pole rides up in the air. He grabs it, a wild grin spreading across his face.

That's when it hits me: he's built a lever, just like we studied in science. Lay a bar (or in this case, a pole) across a pivot point (the firewood), and any power you apply to the long end is multiplied big time at the short. With a large enough lever, you can move just about anything.

Including a Porta-Potti!

I try to shout, "No!" But the word sticks in my throat as Zach heaves down on the pole and the front of the Porta-Potti lurches up off the ground.

A startled shriek comes from inside— Libby's voice, full of fear. I can hear her scrambling to get the door open.

But Zach laughs like a maniac, as if this is just a big joke, a cool prank, and heaves down on the pole again. The Porta-Potti teeters for one horrible second, then begins to slide backward down the hill, picking up speed fast, headed toward the creek.

The grin drops from Zach's face. "Uh-oh," he says.

Libby screams, "Help!"

In a flash I'm out of the tent and running for

all I'm worth. I sprint to the top of the hill and leap onto the Porta-Potti. Which is really moving now. I jerk the door open. Libby locks her eyes onto mine, a look of sheer terror on her face. I grab her and do the only thing I can think of at the moment—bail out—just as the Porta-Potti careens off a rock and veers sideways into the bushes with a giant crash.

It's only after Libby and I roll to a stop, and I'm telling her, "It's okay, you're safe," and trying to get her to quit crying, that I notice the crowd. They heard the commotion and came running. Now they stand all around us with their flashlights shining like one big spotlight. And there I am, wearing nothing but a bunch of underwear. It's my worst nightmare come to life. "Aw, man!" I groan, and cringe, waiting for the Old Me teasing to begin. "Haw! Haw!" they'll say. "Cody's covered in underwear! It's even on his head! Haw! Haw!"

But here's the really cool thing: instead of mean laughter, what I hear is the sound of clapping. Yep, applause. And voices cheering: "Way to go, Cody!" "You did it!" "You saved Libby!" "Yay!"

And the next thing I know, Libby is holding my hands and thanking me over and over again: "Thank you, Cody! Thank you! Thank you! Thank you!" And Amy is gently putting her blanket around my shoulders. And Ms. B is hugging me. And Tyler and Emerson and all the kids in my class are crowding around patting me on the back. They don't care that I'm wearing nothing but a bunch of underwear, even on my head. **Hear Ye, Hear Ye! Listen Up, Everybody!** They like me anyway! And it makes me, Cody Lee Carson, feel like an honest-to-goodness, no-doubt-about-it-this-time, New Me!

Really.

Monday, June 11

I guess if this story had stopped right then and there, it would have just seemed like one of those sloppy, happily-ever-after endings in a Hollywood movie. But like I said before, whoever Mr. Murphy is, he must have been thinking of our Incredible-Fantastic-End-of-the-Year Camp-Out when he came up with Murphy's Law. Not more than two seconds later, there was a big flash of lightning, a boom of thunder, and it was like someone cranked the faucet open full blast. It POURED!

We all ran for our tents, but with it raining

that hard, most of them leaked. Emerson ended up with a lake inside his. And then, of course, it fell down. Just about everybody got soaked, and hardly slept. So we had to cut our Incredible-Fantastic-End-of-the-Year Camp-Out short and go back to Benton early the next morning.

Where Ms. B gave me a C on my stinky feet project. And Zach got into BIG trouble and is probably grounded for the rest of his life. And Emerson sneezed on me and gave me a cold. And MC said, "Gotcha, Mr. Underwear Head!" when she heard how well her and Jordy's suitcase prank had worked. And Mom and Dad made me go to bed at seven o'clock, even though I told them that just because I fell asleep at the dinner table, it didn't mean I was *that* tired. I was just resting my eyes, that's all.

But Mr. Murphy didn't get it all wrong, like he wanted. Libby said she took back everything bad she's ever said about me, even "dork accessory." And Zach wrote Libby a "Sorry About That" letter, telling her that he had just meant to scare her, not send her skiing in a Porta-Potti, and that he was really really sorry, and I could tell he really really meant it. And today all the kids in my class surprised me with a Dress Like Cody Day. They wore underwear on their heads (for a few minutes, anyway, until Ms. B made them take it off), and everybody said it looked cool and maybe that would become the new style. Or maybe not. But anyway, it was funny, and everybody laughed, not at me but with me. And Tyler said, "Let's go swimming together this summer." And last but no way least, today was Amy's birthday. She invited me over for chocolate chip cookie dough ice cream sandwiched between homemade chocolate chip cookies. (Which, in case you didn't know, is the best dessert in the universe.) I got her a really cool gift—a hamster. Its name is Ralphsterina. She liked it so much, she gave me a kiss!

Yep, a real live kiss, not just a chocolate one. I can still feel it, right here on my cheek. Wow!

Can't go on about the love life of Cody Lee Carson anymore, though. I'm out of room in this journal, last page. Way back in September, Ms. B said I should find my true writing voice. Well, I guess this is it. No fancy words out of the thesaurus. No trying to sound like someone I'm not. Just me talking on paper.

Which turned out pretty okay, if I do say so myself. Who knows, I may even send it to one of those New York publishers and see if they'll make it into a book!

Starring Cody Lee *New Me* Carson.

Who, in brilliant-hero-type-guy style, defeats the . . .

ATTACK
OF THE
MUTANT
UNDERWEAR

Acknowledgments

Hear Ye, Hear Ye! Listen Up, Everybody!

I, Tom I-Thought-I'd-Never-Get-This-One-Done Birdseye, have an announcement to make. I am very, *very, VERY* grateful to all the people who helped me turn what began as a fuzzy, vague story idea into this book: Debbie Never-Ending-Support Birdseye, Amy Editor-in-the-Making Birdseye, Kelsey Unique-Perspective Birdseye, Regina Hit-the-Nail-on-the-Head Griffin, John and Kate We-Love-Books Briggs, Dan Stinky-Feet Arp, Gayle Field-Trip Larsen, Connie Always-an-Answer Anderson, Candace Cheerfully-Helpful Hawley, Robert Field-Research Raffield, Dave Gotta-Grant Groth, Chaundra Yay-Kids Smith, Gary Literacy-Man Phillips, and the many inspirational, off-the-wall-wacky kids and wonderful educators I've met in schools around the planet.